CW01496299

What should I do once this story is told? Where should I go? I could go to the police and confess. I could visit a priest and confess. *I ate a person. Is that a sin?*

Praise for *Hunger*

'A feast for the literary senses.'
Anton Hur, judge of the International Booker Prize

'Mesmerising. Inject it into my veins again.'
Irenosen Okojie, author of *Butterfly Fish*

'*Hunger* cuts to the heart. Read at your own peril.'
Frances Cha, author of *If I Had Your Face*

'A book as slender as it is profound. I was enraptured.'
Ling Ling Huang, author of *Natural Beauty*

'A gutting, unforgettable ode to doomed love.
Which is to say, all love.'
Henry Hoke, author of *Open Throat*

'*Hunger* will consume you as you consume it.'
Dean Atta, author of *The Black Flamingo*

'*Hunger* glistens with raw and primal romance.
I could not put it down.'
Jade Song, author of *Chlorine*

'A hefty work of creative genius.'
Barbara Zitwer, author of *The Korean Book of Happiness*

HUNGER

CHOI JIN-YOUNG
TRANSLATED BY SOJE

brazen

June 2025

First edition

First published in Great Britain in 2025 by Brazen, an imprint of
Octopus Publishing Group Ltd
Carmelite House
50 Victoria Embankment
London EC4Y 0DZ
www.octopusbooks.co.uk

An Hachette UK Company
www.hachette.co.uk

The authorised representative in the EEA is Hachette Ireland,
8 Castlecourt Centre, Castleknock Road,
Castleknock, Dublin 15, D15 YF6A, Ireland
email: info@hbgi.ie

Original Korean edition published in 2015 under the title
Guui Jeungmyeong (구의 증명)
This edition published by arrangement with
EunHaeng NaMu Publishing Co., Ltd.,
through Danny Hong Agency and New River Literary Ltd.

Hardback ISBN 978-1-84601-625-7
Trade paperback ISBN 978-1-84091-901-1
eISBN 978-1-84091-903-5

A CIP catalogue record for this book is available from the British Library.

Typeset in 10.5/16pt Swift LT Std by Six Red Marbles UK, Thetford, Norfolk

Printed and bound in Great Britain

3 5 7 9 10 8 6 4 2

MIX
Paper | Supporting
responsible forestry
FSC® C104740

Contents

HUNGER

○

Will humanity last another thousand years?

If anyone reads this, I hope it's a thousand years from the time of writing.

I must live for an extraordinarily long time,
long enough to witness the end of humanity –
which is to say, I want to be the last human alive.
That is my only wish.

I wonder what will shock humans in a thousand years. What will they hate, fear, find humiliating? What will they criticise and mock? Who will they label crazy? Which stories will resonate with them? What will they desire? How will they define beauty and ugliness in a millennium? What about good and evil? Will money still rule the world? What will they eat? What will 'humane' evolve to mean? I want to believe that in a thousand years, humanity will be unrecognisable. No, I hope that in a thousand years, there will be no one left to read or write. Yes, I wish to be the last. That is how long I must hold out.

How long ago was the Bible written? It's been around two thousand years, right? Some are still comforted, moved, even enraptured by these ancient texts. And so they believe. They believe in stories of a child born without sexual intercourse and of a dead man coming back to life, tales that far surpass the wonders of rain falling for forty days or the sea parting in two . . . Faith is the key to grasping absurdity. The ultimate test happens when you're faced with something that makes you want to cry out, *But that doesn't make any sense at all!*

Have faith, and sense will follow.

○

What I need is a resurrection, an immaculate conception. A miracle beyond the bounds of science and ethics. A thousand-year leap through time. I need Armageddon or eternal life. I need to lose my head. I don't need to be human – I just need you.

Faith is what I need.

What should I do once this story is told? What could I possibly do? Where should I go? I could go to the police and confess. I could visit a priest and confess. *I ate a person. A human being. Is that a sin?* They'll do with me as they see fit. I could say whatever they tell me to say, go wherever they tell me to go.

To tell this story, and to live on:

that is all I want.

○

Gu died on the street.

He looked no different from a passed-out drunk.

I sat there, cradling him in my arms, waiting for dawn.

The wind carried the scent of new clothes.

My mind tossed and turned like an insomniac in the dead of night.

It's going to rain.

What do I do?

Rain would be good.

No, not yet . . .

I stroked Gu's hair, brittle and unruly down to his collarbones. A clump came loose. I examined it in my hand, rolled it into a ball and swallowed it whole. I couldn't bear to lose any part of him. The night stretched on without a drop of rain. I did not cry; Gu did not breathe. Even with his lifeless weight in my arms, I couldn't comprehend that he was truly gone. His physicality and the notion of death seemed to repel each other, like poles of a magnet. Had I imagined it all? Nothing felt real, even weeks after dragging his stiffening body back home.

I knew you'd come.

I knew you would, and I waited for you. But I couldn't decide when I wanted you to get here – before or after my end. You always complained that I never knew what I wanted, making you decide for me. And here I was, face to face with death and still figuring myself out.

I decided you shouldn't have to watch me die. I didn't want to leave you with a wound more painful and permanent than my absence. Besides, I had nothing more to say. Or so I thought. I convinced myself that, over the years, I had said everything I needed to. Even if I'd missed something, there was no need to speak it now. Some things are better left unsaid. I thought you knew me well enough to understand. But was I right? Had I really said everything I needed to say? No, who am I kidding? You should have been here, by my side. With my last breath, I realised what I had wanted all along.

I wanted to see you.

Not the old, weathered payphone, not some stubborn weed pushing through the grimy pavement. Not a lonesome cross piercing the foggy dusk. You were what I wanted to see. Do you even know that? Or can you not know because I never told you? The thought of you not knowing kills me. I died with thoughts of you, but without glimpsing you one last time. You should've come a little sooner. My final vision of this world should've been you.

I noticed the light pooled beneath a street lamp at the head of the alley.

I looked at it until my eyes drifted shut.

Dam will be here any moment now.

That light looks so inviting, so warm.

Warm like Dam.

It's not that I'd never thought about it before. Gu was always on the run, sometimes disappearing for days at a time. The nights he was with me, Gu collapsed from exhaustion like a withered chrysanthemum. An unspoken question hung in the air.

What if he dies first?

I resolved that, if it came to that, I would follow him. But what would become of our bodies, I wondered. Who would tend to us? A public servant would probably collect and dispose of us without giving a second thought to the kind of lives we led, what we meant to each other, the memories etched into our skin. They'd simply burn us like roadkill. Gone – just like that. I could accept this end for myself, but not for Gu. I would have to hide his body before taking my own life; that was my revised plan.

I refused to dwell on these dark thoughts. Then one day, when we hid in an abandoned house, scarred and split like an old oak struck by lightning, Gu broached the subject of death. Lying on his side, he pulled me close.

—Are you hungry?

I shook my head.

—Are you tired?

I nodded.

—Did you weep at your aunt's funeral?

I held my tongue.

—Do you want to visit her?

Gu hadn't been around when she passed away. I resented him for this, but ultimately decided against holding a grudge. Let bygones be bygones, I resolved.

—What will you do when I die?

The question alone made me want to cry. How cruel of him to ask.

—I'll leave you enough money to cremate or bury me. Turns out even dying's expensive. But you'll have to keep it on the down-low, or else the fuckers will sell off my corpse.

I sat up to take a better look at him. His gentle eyes and handsome nose, his cute ears. His dry, flaky skin that I longed to lick clean. His sad pecs, nice bum and rail-thin legs. I caressed him all over. How could I ever burn or bury such a beautiful body? How could I let that happen?

—I won't be able to do it, so please don't die before me.

—I feel the same, Dam. But it will happen one day. Should I just disappear and die by myself? Would that be better?

—That's the worst thing you could do. Why don't we shelve this conversation and focus on everything we want to do together while we're still here? Once we're feeling better, we'll joke about the morbid stuff and laugh off death like it's nothing.

As I lay back down, Gu spoke again.

—If you die before me, I will eat you.

I take back what I said about hiding his body before killing myself. A ridiculous idea that could only make sense while Gu was still alive. Hide him where? I couldn't even keep him safe in life. And suicide? Idiotic. No, I have a better plan.

I will eat you, Gu.

I will eat you and live for an extraordinarily long time. I will outlive those who treated us as less than human. Even as they grow old, fall ill, die – until they are long forgotten and their bodies disintegrate into nothingness – I will live. I will carry your remains with me to the very end of time. You will die only when I die. I won't follow you into death; I will have you follow me.

I won't watch you disappear.

I will live.

I will live to remember you.

◯

Before I met my aunt, I lived with my grandfather. When he passed away, she gave up her life as a Buddhist nun in a mountain-top temple and came down to meet me. Neither of us knew of the other's existence; his death brought us together.

So the aunt hadn't known she was an aunt, and the niece hadn't known she was a niece.

Auntie had no idea how I came into the world, or how I ended up living with my grandfather. Neither did I. Grandpa took his secret to the grave. I think he had meant to say something to someone, but death took him by surprise. So both Auntie and I remained in the dark. We got by on our wits, without knowing the basic facts and oblivious to our own ignorance. Some secrets are better left undiscovered. Thinking too much only messes with you and brings on headaches. You might end up questioning your entire existence.

After leaving the temple, Auntie got a job assembling products in buildings made from shipping containers.

—What did you make today?

—I made sounds.

This meant she'd made speakers.

—What about today?

—Scents.

Air-fresheners, obviously.

—And today?

—I made beauty.

Hand mirrors. It took me a while to get that one.

—What about this time?

—I made darkness.

Light bulbs. This one too I didn't understand. I pressed her about this 'darkness', wanting to know what she meant, until she finally snapped at me. I burst into tears.

—Is it so sinful to not know something?

—Sometimes what you need is time, not an easy answer. The things you don't understand now will start to make sense in time. Ignorance isn't a sin, but impatience can be.

Stunned, I fired back:

—What if I dropped dead right this second? I'd die without knowing!

Her eyes widened in shock. We fell into a loud silence, probably thinking of Grandpa who symbolised death for us.

—Let's not do this, Dam.

She sighed and turned away, but I wanted to keep talking. Conversation was my only outlet and means of expressing my love for her.

Back then, Auntie was the only person I loved. I poured all my affection into her hoping for the same in return, but she was always working. Putting food on the table was how she expressed her love.

○

To suffer is to experience physical or emotional pain.

There can be no love without suffering.

Gu and I were in the same class for two years. I have no memory of our first year together, but when we turned nine, Gu began bullying me. He would steal my backpack, pull my hair, fling my school slippers across the classroom, scribble all over my notebooks and kick my chair. The torment was all physical; he never said a single word. If our paths crossed on the days I got a maths problem wrong or got left out, the days I watched the clouds bloom like flowers across a clear blue sky, I would quietly let a few tears fall. One day, Gu caught me crying and scowled. He fixed his gaze on me or something behind me, who knows, and then muttered something indecipherable. Was it 'fuck off', 'for real', 'stop it', or 'sorry'? I spent the entire day micro-analysing those two syllables.

I didn't hate Gu, my little tormentor.

I was just a little resentful.

A part of me longed to say something, but I could scarcely

meet his eyes, let alone say his name. When he pulled my hair, I looked at him from the corner of my eye; when he flicked my eraser off the desk, I stole another glance; and when he kicked my chair, I simply watched him walk away. We turned ten without having ever called each other by name.

Gu lived less than ten minutes from me, meaning that we walked the same streets, swung on the same swings, soaked at the same bathhouse. Yet we rarely crossed paths outside of school. Still, I would look around, hoping to see him, only to feel an unfamiliar disappointment gnawing at my heart. One afternoon, by some twist of fate, I called in sick on the very day he too decided to skip school. We finally ran into each other in an empty alley, stopping in our tracks and smiling awkwardly.

    —Why are you here?
    —Why are *you* here?
    Despite the interrogation, we were secretly thrilled.

Of course, this wasn't our first encounter.

Neither of us recalled how we first met at eight years old, but we treasured our memory of the first time we called each other by name. I remember every detail: the languid sunlight of midday, the lilac-laced breeze swirling around us, Gu's blue work jacket smelling faintly of coal briquettes. *Why are you here?* he had asked, wiping his palms on his trousers and kicking the ground as if trying to unearth my answer.

*

From then on, I found room in my heart for Gu and began to love him just as I loved Auntie. And they loved sharing my love.

Back then Auntie was making summer. I remember her telling me so.

What summer meant, I've forgotten.

We became inseparable, indulging in sugar together day and night.

I went to Dam's house almost every day after school. Without the pocket money to fund an afternoon snack, she would retrieve a bag of white sugar from the cupboard and carefully tip some into my cupped hands. Then we would sit against the kitchen sink, licking sugar off the tips of our moistened index fingers.

—What if your aunt finds out?

—Just say we got the hiccups.

Dam always had an answer.

Again and again we dipped our fingers into the sugar, until the day Dam bought us ice cream with money she'd found in her aunt's trouser pocket. I didn't ask if she had permission to go through her aunt's closet. I instinctively knew we were stealing and didn't want to embarrass her, but what if her aunt eventually caught on? Should I confess my part, or play dumb? I felt sick just thinking about it, and I didn't have the heart to stop Dam. The last thing I wanted was for her to feel bad. Dam wasn't a bad kid. She was my favourite person in the world, and I loved spending time with her. I wanted to do whatever she did, go wherever she went. I wanted us to be together without the labels of 'good' or 'bad', 'right' and 'wrong' – without deciding who was the better person.

Once a day we rifled through her aunt's closet for loose cash. We were easily excited and easily disappointed. One time, I struck gold before Dam. She studied the note in my hand.

—Put it back. I'll do it myself.

—It doesn't matter who does it. It's still stealing.

I'd never called it stealing before, and I instantly regretted it.

—Right. So don't do it.

—Why?

—I just don't want you to.

—So you can but I can't?

We locked eyes.

—I'll do it for us both.

—I don't want you doing anything I shouldn't do.

Dam snatched the banknote from my unsuspecting hand and returned it to the jacket. For a moment she glared at the pocket or sleeve, who knows. I wiped my sweaty palms on my thighs before awkwardly reaching for her hand.

We waited for nightfall lying side by side, our stomachs rumbling in protest. Before long, Dam's aunt would return from work. Or my mum would call, summoning me back to my own home.

The night came slowly, as if the last of the light was scrutinising us, putting us to the test.

We were in our twenties when I brought up our childhood habit of theft.

—Honestly, I hated lying to Auntie. I felt worse for acting innocent than the actual stealing.

Silence settled between us. Dam looked sad, probably remembering her aunt. My mind drifted to Noma. Maybe Dam was remembering him too. After Noma left us, we never spoke his name again. Maybe we just couldn't. I wanted to ask Dam if she thought we were partly to blame. But had she asked me the question . . . I wouldn't have known what to say. So I couldn't bring myself to ask her.

Maybe, I thought, I'll find out when I die.

Maybe all those questions will finally find answers.

But what do I know, really? Turns out we're as clueless in death as in life. The only difference is the dead don't agonise over the unknown. They know to leave some things alone.

If Dam asked me now, about Noma, I'd tell her it wasn't our fault. I'd try to ease her suffering.

The summer I turned nineteen, I stole again. A T-shirt from the neighbour's clothes line. It was white, with the red Levi's logo emblazoned across the chest, a stretched-out collar and yellowed armpits. I wanted it worn-in, to look like someone who had grown up in designer brands. I envied people who treated expensive clothes like leisurewear.

That was the only thing I ever stole.

Yet I somehow found myself buried in debt, owing money I'd never seen or touched.

I tried running and ended up here.

A realm of nothingness. A formless void without field, sea, sky – and yet, I can feel you. With every cell of me. I feel you, right here, but you are not here. Or maybe I'm not here? But I am. I am here, and so are you. And I am also not here, and neither are you.

Dam is here.

And here is a world without Dam.

As the dark began to lift into the blue of dawn, I hailed a cab with Gu on my back. I kept an eye on the driver, making a show of attempting to wake Gu and sighing audibly. He played his part as a drunk passed out against me. I feared the driver might offer to help carry Gu to the front door, but naturally, he did not. After placing Gu inside our room, I set water to boil. I dragged a large plastic basin in from the backyard and scrubbed it clean. On colder days, Gu and I used to fill it with warm water and bathe together. We nestled, tenderly tracing each other's backs and marvelling at the clouds of white steam blooming from our heads, shoulders and fingers.

—What if our bodies evaporate into thin air, like in that legend?

—There's a legend like that?

—Isn't there? Well, we can always make one.

The water would soon cool, leaving us shivering and our teeth chattering again.

*

Ever so gently, I undressed Gu and placed him in the basin. I, too, entered bare. Slowly, I washed him. And as I did, I held him. I feared I would scar him, with even the lightest touch dimpling his skin. I changed the water multiple times and rinsed him clean before patting him dry. I lay him flat and swabbed every inch of him with rubbing alcohol – the insides of his mouth, his nostrils, his belly button, all of it. I clipped his fingernails and toenails, and then swept the clippings into my mouth. I combed his hair and swallowed the strands that fell out. There was even less left of my little Gu now. I sat against the wall and looked at him. His body like a dimming candle.

No one can know.
No one can know Gu died.

They won't care. They won't mourn his passing or remember his life, not for even a second. Some of them might even say he's better off. Say his life was barely a life at all, that it was going nowhere. He had heard it all when he was alive. I could not let him hear it again in death. How could they say his death was for the best? How dare they? If those loan sharks find out, they'll try to sell him for parts, no doubt. They'll claim his corpse and sell it off like a slab of meat.

Gu has to stay alive in their minds. I'll make those guys search and search for him until they are driven insane. Why should I report his death? For what purpose? For who? I can't do it, not when he's right here, right in front of me, with this beautiful body that I can touch, that I can hold.

No one can know.

No one cared about him anyway. They put a price on his life, used him and discarded him, and then acted like he never existed. How can someone who never existed cease to exist?

I can't bury or burn his beautiful body.

Gu is here. Right in front of me.

○

We grew up at the same pace. I loved how Gu was just like me, neither taller nor shorter but experiencing the world from the same vantage point. The way he would sit through my prattling, occasionally nodding as he looked off into the distance, gave me butterflies. It made the crown of my head tingle.

We were twelve when the bullying started.

—Eww, look at them holding hands! I heard they even kiss and touch each other down there.

We were immediately cast out. No one wanted to talk or play with us, but they were happy to use us like an X-rated comic passed around the school.

The rumours became increasingly bizarre.

Allegedly, we drank, smoked, stole from Gu's parents, and when caught doing so, proceeded to set their house on fire. When it was revealed that both his parents' house and store were still standing, the story was revised from 'the house burned down' to 'the house *almost* burned down'. In short, we had at least attempted arson.

*

Gu and I stayed together through it all.

The daily taunts infuriated me, but never enough to stay away from my Gu. It wasn't until a big fight broke out between him and a bully, with the bully's older brother and friends getting involved, that the rumours reached adult ears. Our form teacher and Gu's parents, though fully aware of the nature of our relationship, still interrogated us as if we were dirty.

We had shared ladles of plum wine.
We had pretended to smoke with cigarette butts taken from
    a piled ashtray.
We had stolen money for ice cream.
We had slept beside each other countless times.

As we stood there blankly, hand in hand, neither confirming nor denying the accusations, our teacher demanded that we let go. Or maybe it was Gu's mother, I can't remember.

—You should be ashamed of yourselves. You're too old to be going around holding hands. It's time you both started playing with the other children.

Wait, weren't we the ones being bullied? Did the adults just take things at face value? If Gu hadn't fought back, what would've happened to us? How much bigger would the rumours have grown?

More importantly, why did Gu drop my hand at that very moment?

*

A wave of shame washed over me. Without his hand, every rumour seemed to become true and taint our time together. It was like giving in to the mockery. I felt scared and alone, as if thrown naked into the middle of a crowded square. Then came the anger.

What led up to the fist fight was more than just the teasing.

While on cleaning duty one day, I noticed Deoji sitting on the windowsill, eyeing something. I followed his gaze to Dam, who was rearranging the desks after sweeping and mopping the floor. Deoji chewed on his bottom lip, still staring.

I couldn't stand the way he looked at her.

I had never considered that someone might desire Dam like that. Maybe the bullies actually had a huge crush on her. Deoji's eyes stayed glued to Dam even as she scanned the room for me. She briefly met his gaze before turning away, pretending not to see him, but Deoji stomped over to make gross comments about her body. A couple of kids snickered and joined in.

I hated the way they were all looking at her.

I didn't know what to do. If I went to her side, it would only get worse. But if I didn't, she'd have to face their stares alone. I stood there, paralysed by indecision, until she spotted me and walked over without a moment's hesitation. That's how it was with us. Dam always made the first move. She never left me hanging.

*

A few moments before our fight, Deoji came up to me and started mouthing off about Dam.

—Heard you two fuck like rabbits. I bet that bitch screeches like a dog when you strip her down, tie her up and fuck her with your tiny cock.

I'd never heard words like that in my life, but I knew they meant Deoji had been fantasising about Dam. As he sat there, chewing his lip and watching her, his thoughts had wandered into fantasies wilder than the rumours of us smoking cigarettes, sniffing glue and setting things on fire. I'd never been more disgusted. I had no choice but to fight him.

It didn't matter that I was smaller and weaker than Deoji. I was ready to take a hundred, a thousand punches, anything to shut his stupid eyes. I needed to smash his head in, claw out his eyeballs and wring his brain dry of any thoughts of Dam. But before I could even get a swing in, Deoji's brother and friends swept in like D'Artagnan and the Three Musketeers. They beat the shit out of me. I took so many punches I thought I'd die, but I didn't. I kept getting hit.

Out of the corner of my eye, I saw Dam.

Her face was bright red as she screamed, cried, implored them to stop. The blows continued unabated. I watched Dam pick up a chair. *Don't*, I wanted to shout, *Don't get involved, just walk away*, but I could barely speak with the blood in my mouth. The last thing I wanted was for Dam to see me like that or, God forbid, fight for me. It was just too much. As soon as she swung the chair, Deoji grabbed it and tossed it aside. He turned to Dam.

—This is none of your business.

—You worthless pieces of shit!

—Shut up and get the fuck out of here.

Deoji's brother grabbed a fistful of my hair and with it, dragged me around the room.

Things went from bad to worse when the sixth graders got involved. Our mums were called in. Deoji's bowed respectfully to the form teacher, who returned the gesture. My mum, on the other hand, wasted no time on formalities and got straight to yelling at me.

—You little rascal, why the hell have you started getting into fights? You scared the living daylights out of me!

It was nothing I hadn't heard before. I knew that she was putting on a show for them, but her words still got to me. Deoji's mum had draped herself in a long black fur coat that looked so silky and soft I almost reached out to touch it. She shrugged it off to reveal a pristine white blouse adorned with pearl buttons and lace trim, paired with a navy skirt. Her outfit was immaculate – not a loose thread or speck of dust to be found. I could tell she had a nice tan. My mum was much paler from sitting indoors, ringing up customers' purchases and counting their change all day. My mum was beautiful. People told her that as often as they asked, *How much is this?* Dam was also beautiful. That must be why Deoji was eyeing her, chewing on his lip like that.

A new feeling came over me as Deoji's mum demanded that Dam and I let go of each other's hand.

Am I allowed to like Dam?

Wouldn't it be better if Deoji liked her?

I keep getting Dam in trouble. It was Deoji who stopped her throwing that chair. Not me.

My head spinning, I let go of her hand. Dam stared at me, stunned, as if a bomb had just detonated. When she reached for my hand again, I attempted a fist but couldn't clench it shut. Dam wrapped her hand around mine, squeezing hard, before letting go in anger. She tried again to pry my fist open but eventually gave up.

After that, we went right back to passing each other without a second glance. Whenever we crossed paths, or she crossed my mind, I'd recite my new mantra:

I'm trouble. I'm not good for her.

○

The cold persisted, preserving a thick sheen of ice on the ground that refused to melt. Our bodies grew small and stiff. I lay facing Gu and listened to the songbirds, the cockerels, the wind. The room was cold as stone and enveloped in darkness. I couldn't keep myself awake long. Once, I cracked the door open to snowflakes falling like flower petals. The night sky was strangely bright without a moon or star in sight. *No, it's not light outside. It's dark inside*, I muttered, hoping to wake Gu. I wanted him to say something, anything, even whine about the cold or order me to shut the door. I boiled water. I drank some and used the rest to wipe him down with a towel. I consumed everything that fell away: skin, hair, nails. Then I swabbed his body with rubbing alcohol again. I pressed my ear to his stomach and closed my eyes, hoping for sound. I missed his voice. How could I live without its music? I rested my head on him, tasting my own tears, until I thought I felt him take a breath. I opened my eyes to his penis. All night long I stroked and sucked on it, before finally biting in.

○

The damp air hung heavy with the promise of rain. Sweat trickled from the nape of my neck down my back. I wiped it away and looked up at the sky. A lump formed in my throat. Friends, school, my future – none of it mattered.

I barely saw Gu in secondary school.

His absence did nothing to stop my obsession. I replayed our time together, wondering what he might be doing now and if I ever crossed his mind. My thoughts circled until they eventually turned against him. It didn't occur to me to think about anything or anyone else, let alone focus on homework or making new friends. My brain registered nothing but Gu. It was only when my thoughts of him began to fade, and new ones took shape, that I realised.

Gu was everything.

Nothing could touch the depth and intensity of his existence.

*

Adrift in missing him, my feet instinctively led me to his house. No sound came from behind the rusty gate. *Should I wait? What if he comes out? What should I say? How's it going? Life is boring without you?* My head buzzed as I silently called out to Gu, but neither the house nor the street answered.

Gu must have forgotten about me.

Of course he had. If we really shared a special bond, how could he not sense my soul's call? The sky let fall raindrops as large as hailstones, the splatter forming circles in the muddy road as if to say *yes, yes* to my suspicions. Yet I couldn't stop obsessing. As I walked home, I wondered what I would do if Gu were to suddenly materialise. And then, there he was, standing at my front door, just as I had stood in front of his moments earlier.

　　—Gu.

　　He turned around slowly.

　　—How long have you been standing here?

　　He sighed softly.

　　—I should ask you the same.

●

I often found myself standing outside Dam's house.

I was now a young man, and sharing a small room with my parents had become a bit awkward. Too proud to cry or pretend to sleep through their fights, I spent many nights alone in a tiny room attached to the store. Lying on the floor, I thought of Dam. Listening to my parents argue, I thought of Dam. Eating radish kimchi with white rice, I thought of Dam. Watching the sky change colours at dusk, hearing faint footsteps in the alley at night, or feeling myself get hard in the early hours, I thought of Dam. I walked to her house and silently called out to her night after night, as if keeping a journal, every page scrawled with my steps to Dam.

Does she ever think of me?
    If she did, she would know I was here.
    But she didn't. She never came outside, not once in all those nights.

I guess she's forgotten me.

I doubt she thinks about me before bed.
She probably sleeps like a baby.
I convinced myself of it.

I was both comforted and crushed that she was sleeping so well. I guess I still couldn't figure myself out, but Dam would get it. She helped me understand myself.

I wasted countless spring nights wandering in circles, watching new blooms wilt and get trampled underfoot.

The first day of the monsoon season, with the rain starting to wash away the perfume of the flowers, I found Dam standing at my front door, just as I had stood at hers the day before. I was torn between joy and heartbreak, knowing too well what must be running through her head.

●

Sure, we patched things up – but something had shifted. We could no longer walk hand in hand, lie side by side, or spend every waking moment together. Something held me back.

I could tell at first glance that she had changed.

Her breasts looked like she had stuffed two choco pies down her shirt. Her arms, thighs and bum had filled out. Her neck had grown longer and slimmer. It was like going to a theme park. *Does she get periods?* I didn't dare ask. I felt strangely cut off from her changed body and, honestly, a little intimidated by it.

I couldn't even look her in the eye.

Where she had grown into a woman, I remained short, scrawny and weak. I wasn't as good at football and basketball as the other boys, but I was a strong cyclist. I could pedal for hours without stopping, no matter how tired I was.

When Mum asked where I was going at night, I'd either say I was getting some air or not respond at all. It didn't matter if she was suspicious, indifferent or happy for me – I wanted to keep my relationship with Dam private. What other people thought of us always felt slightly out of sync with our reality.

Dam wasn't as chatty as she once was. Her words now carried a note of callousness. Like: *Our English teacher is soo cool. He picks me to read out loud all the time. He's only ten years older than us.* Or: *Hyoseok keeps calling my phone.*

Then she started freaking out about her weight, grabbing at her stomach and insisting that she was fat under her clothes, my reassurances falling on stony ground. Meanwhile, I focused on her bra straps underneath the thin white fabric of our summer uniforms, and with a squint, could even make out the design and colour. Taking note of her bare legs, I couldn't help but wonder if she was wearing anything but panties underneath her skirt. Occasionally, her arm would brush against mine and leave me shivering in the middle of summer. Dam had developed a habit of running her fingers through her bobbed hair before tying it up into a ponytail, releasing the scent of her floral shampoo laced with her sweat. I watched the beads slip from behind her ear down to her collarbones as she fanned herself lazily with one hand. Her lips looked as slick as an eel. Her skin as pale, firm and dewy as a freshly peeled chestnut.

It was all too much.

Every detail about Dam sent me flying over the edge. I imagined her naked skin every time I laid eyes on her, and when I didn't. The guiltier I felt, the bolder my imagination grew. I could barely look her in the eye, but there was no inch of her I hadn't already tasted in my mind. Desire and shame wrestled within me. It pained me to look, and it pained me to look away. I wanted to get closer, and I feared being closer. I had to remain on my very best behaviour.

Dam, on the other hand, was as nonchalant as ever. She had this breezy, carefree way about her, like she'd just stepped out for a casual stroll in the fields.

It crushed me. And it comforted me.

Gu had changed a lot.

He spoke less and his voice was weaker. Even his actions were, how to put it, oddly stunted. It was as if the rest of his body had continued growing and forgotten his heart somewhere inside, like a huge sheet of paper crumpled into a tiny ball. He was never the extroverted type, but he used to speak his mind when needed. Now, it was as if his entire being had been soundproofed. It broke my heart.

I wished he'd let the walls down for me.

Auntie was thrilled about our reconciliation and didn't hesitate to offer her unsolicited advice.

—You can't be glued together like before. A peck on the cheek is fine, but things can easily get out of hand now that you're teenagers. If anything happens, you need to tell me right away.

I got her worries; I was also worried, but for the opposite reason. Gu was acting like a perfect priest. He wouldn't budge an inch, not even to hold hands. I fantasised about linking arms and leaning on his shoulder. Kissing was another world altogether, as distant as the stars in the night sky.

Auntie had no idea what I was going through.

And so, without any real justification, she became the unwitting target of my frustrations. I resolved to never tell her anything about my relationship with Gu. Whatever happened between us, stayed between us. That's how it was with us. But as Auntie's suspicions grew, Gu remained uninterested in creating any secrets with me – a sharp blow to my ego. In retaliation, I began saying things I knew would make him jealous. I wasn't actively trying to hurt him, but I wasn't not trying to hurt him. I don't know, I was a mess back then.

The winter after graduating middle school, I went in for a kiss. I aimed for a tender moment like I'd seen on TV but ended up nearly sucking his face off. He stepped back, stumbling further into a dead-end alley until his back hit the wall. With nowhere to go, he slowly slid to the ground. I followed and kissed him again. I have no idea how long we stayed there, feverishly exploring each other's mouths like there was no tomorrow. Then Gu moaned in pain. I figured his lips were sore, just like mine, but it hurt so good I didn't even mind the taste of blood. I traced his lips with my finger. *Not there*, Gu breathed. He adjusted himself before abruptly walking away. Back then, I knew nothing about erections. The way a penis could lengthen and harden was far beyond my imagination. It wasn't until secondary school that I learned the anatomical details.

Eventually, I shared my belated realisation with him. My giggles soon became moans as he slid inside me with very little resistance. Even though we knew we belonged to each other, and even when we had time to waste, we couldn't help but rush. As if we might be interrupted or separated at any moment. With his trousers barely down his legs, he'd insert himself as soon as I'd spread mine. Our lips never parted as we writhed against each other, knocking teeth and slobbering everywhere, wrestling and pinning each other down with screams. Nothing could separate us: not the walls, nor the floors, not even our own bodies. We were one.

Our nights together, everything from our first kiss, were secrets kept between us. Now, I keep them alone.

●

I always lost weight in my lower body first. Before dying, my thighs had become as thin as my calves. *You're like a twig*, Dam would pout and lovingly massage my legs with her small hands. *A man should have thick thighs.* She liked to rest her head on my lap, periodically rolling over to sniff my stomach or suck me off. During sex, she would straddle me and hold on tight with all four limbs. It wasn't my favourite position, but I liked watching her gazelle neck and waist arch back. Our bodies intertwined, becoming one. Our writhing, both thrilling and pathetic. I drank in the view, her eyes rolling back in pleasure. I wanted to feel all of her with all of me. I wanted her to exist on top of me.

And now she's eating me, crying. Was that blood or pus running down her face? Did she realise she was crying? Could she feel me watching, listening? I used to think death was the end, but my mind is still here. I wish I could take the burden of my body with me and leave her only my heart. I wish she could eat my love for her. I remember everything: our first kiss, so sweet and silly, and all the nights spent reminiscing about it.

Here, I remember you because that's all I can do.
These memories are my future.
These memories of you.
My future is you.

○

Gu got a job as soon as he turned seventeen. After evening study hours at school, I would station myself outside the factory and wait. Sometimes he surfaced as I arrived; other times, I loitered for over an hour.

In reality, the wait began not at the factory gates but from the moment he left my side.

My heart was on permanent standby, no matter where I was or what I was doing. I waited all day long, knowing perfectly well when we'd agreed to meet. Even when we were together, I was waiting for him. And even when he was the one waiting for me, I was still waiting for him.

Does loving someone mean waiting forever?
     Even now, with Gu dead, I find myself waiting for him.
     Is he waiting for me?

He wasn't back then. Gu was always working. He sorted vegetables at a supermarket before dawn, went to school during the daytime, and loaded and unloaded trucks until midnight. At the weekend, he split himself between two convenience stores. I had no idea how anyone could sustain this lifestyle, but somehow, Gu made it work. The twenty minutes it took to walk home from the factory was the only time we had to ourselves. The moment he appeared dragging his bike, the first smile of the day would break across my face. I'd take my place on the back of the bike and wrap my arms around his waist, breathing in his warmth and his scent.

—Aren't you tired?

—I'm okay.

He always said he was 'okay'. I eventually banned the word.

I asked him which job was the hardest. The convenience store gig, he decided, because all the standing around led his mind to wander anxiously. And he didn't like handling cash. Why was he holding in his piss through peak hours when not even a tenth of the money coming in would reach his pockets?

—Working with my hands clears my head, but the time goes by way too fast.

—Isn't that a good thing?

—It scares me, how life is passing me by.

He hesitated.

—Like I'll wake up one day and it'll all be over.

—Never. It'll be okay.

I made sure to speak without hesitating, but a person can work themselves to an early death. This, I know now.

—I don't hate working. I just don't want work to be the only thing I do, you know. I don't want to live like this forever.

His voice trembled, more frightened than exasperated.

—We just have to get through this bit. It'll be different when we're adults. It'll be okay.

I was breaking my own ban.

Did I say the wrong thing?

Should I not have said that?

What should I have said?

He was facing the world, and I was facing his back. *Fuck living to work. We won't end up like those people.* Would those words have helped him? They did nothing for me. Besides, I had no interest in the future. The moments spent holding him, leaning on his back, were enough. I needed nothing more.

Joy led us to sadness.

Noma was six years younger than us. He skipped over to the factory after his after-school tutoring sessions to see his parents who worked day and night, his backpack bouncing on his back. Noma waited patiently in the small office doing homework, eating and warming his hands by the heater. The other workers weren't particularly fond of him, but they weren't bothered by him either. They'd catch glimpses of the boy slinking around like a stray cat and think of their own children in after-school classes, with granny, or watching TV. Emotions were left at the factory door. The machines were indifferent to humans, and fatal accidents could happen in the blink of an eye.

Noma's parents tried to keep him out of the way, but he wouldn't be deterred.

—I'll be quiet. I'll behave, I promise. I won't be any trouble.

He rattled off his lines whenever anyone so much as glanced in his general direction, like a robot.

*

—You really like it here, don't you?

Noma peered at me, probably sizing me up, before giving me a curt nod. I put on my best casual voice.

—Do you, Noma?

He was silent for a long time.

—There are no kids here.

—Kids? What kids? You mean your friends?

Without a word, Noma whipped out a beat-up workbook from his backpack. In the upper right corner of each page sat a small drawing. A flip book. He gave me permission to flick through.

A boy with his head hanging low
slowly lifting his right arm
raising his fist high
and giving a thumbs up
bigger than his own head.

I let out a laugh. Noma smirked.

I took him home whenever his parents were required overnight, teaching him how to ride the bike. He got the hang of it quickly, taking only a few tumbles before pedalling alone with us walking either side. Some nights, Dam and Noma would walk hand in hand and leave me to push. The bike seemed almost alive, as if it might cycle off by itself. I let go, and it fell. I let go again, and again, it fell. We giggled like fools every time it fell.

Noma would doodle in every single one of his school workbooks. I waited impatiently for him to get through the modules and unveil his latest creations.

Two eyes morphing into weird shapes spelling out 'EYES

OFF'. A ribbon unravelling to reveal a massive turd shooting out of a gift box. In another, the sun, the moon and a star converging to form the three hands of a melting clock. In yet another, a person picking their ear to unearth a second turd, a knife, a flower and a diamond. Finally, a man, a woman, a boy and a bicycle fading into the distance until they are stars.

Our walks had a quiet warmth to them. Noma between us made me feel safe and soothed my nerves, as if an angel were watching over us. Or as if we were looking out for each other, wrapped in the arms of the night. They plucked the thorns out of my heart. They made me a better person. We licked ice cream in the summer and munched bungeoppang in the winter, losing ourselves in the beauty of the spring flowers and autumn leaves. At the end of the night, I'd wait for Noma to lock his door and kiss Dam goodbye. Then it was a shower and four to five hours of sleep before doing it all again, but there was a warm ball of rice in my heart that exhaustion and the future could never spoil.

Once, I asked Noma a question I couldn't answer myself.
　　—What do you want to be when you grow up?
　　The scariest question of all.
　　—What do *you* want to be when you grow up?
　　Touché. I took the coward's way out.
　　—You go first.
　　—I'm going to be a good dad.
　　—A good dad?
　　—Yeah. The bestest dad in the world.
　　—What kind of dad is the bestest dad in the world?

—The bestest husband makes the bestest dad. Duh.

—Is that what your mum says?

He rummaged through his bag, ignoring me.

Our Noma. The bestest kid in the world.

One of those nights, Noma was riding the bike with us walking either side. He matched our pace, wiggling the handlebars and zigzagging, pedalling backwards. He had grown taller that year; we remained unchanged. Everyone's faces, fingers and toes throbbed with cold that winter.

—I have to finish this new workbook over the break. The teacher hit me for drawing in them, but I'll show you guys before rubbing everything out.

The thought of him erasing the drawings, the small curls of rubber piling up, really got to me.

—What will you draw this time?

—Something super sexy. I'm going to erase it anyway.

I wondered what Noma's idea of 'sexy' was. It probably wasn't any different to mine.

—Hey, when did you guys start liking each other?

—When we were younger than you are now.

—How did you become friends?

—We just did, naturally.

—What do you mean, 'naturally'?

Noma braked so dramatically the bike swerved to the right. I was the only one who startled.

—Want me to push you?

Noma ignored Gu's offer.

—Dad promised he'll buy me a bike in secondary school.

The boys his age biked to and from school, no matter where they lived. Hundreds of bikes stood parked in a corner of the schoolyard. They looked like notes on a staff.

—When I get my bike, I'm going far. All the way to the ocean.

—Maybe wait until you're a bit older.

Gu patted Noma's back.

—Okay but how do you get close to someone 'naturally'?

Noma wasn't done.

When you really like someone, there's nowhere to hide it from them, I almost blurted out.

—You two are dating, right?

Gu and I laughed drily. We were well beyond 'dating'.

—The kids at school are dating too.

It had been months since graduation, but one of our bullies still hit up my phone.

—They're not like you guys though. They're dumb.

The bike swerved again, this time to the left. Gu barely caught it.

—So, who do you want to be dumb with?

Gu was joking, but Noma's face grew grave.

—It's not like that. I just want someone to be nice to me.

Noma pedalled hands-free, ours steadying the bars.

—So I can be nice back.

It was undeniable: the boy was experiencing his first crush.

Our usual spot grew in the distance. It was right before closing, meaning the vendor lady would either give us the leftovers for free or be all out. We always placed bets on how many bungeoppang remained. *Three*, Noma guessed. Gu seconded. *None today*, I predicted.

And there were none. We lay claim to the remaining fish cake skewers. *Tomorrow, I'm going to stuff my face with bungeoppang*, Noma muttered between mouthfuls. Gu scooped some broth into a paper cup, handing it to him. I tore off a tissue and wiped his mouth. *Thanks*, Noma said. It was unusual to be thanked; we'd never thanked each other for the small things before. After we paid and left the stall, I licked some soy sauce smeared on Gu's hand. He gave me a shy smile, and I probably returned a dumb joke. Noma looked back at us, securing his left foot on the pedal before swinging his right leg over the seat. Then he skidded forward. That's how I remember it at least. After a thunderous crack that seemed to split the Earth in two, Noma flew up into the air.

In the end, his growth spurt mattered little. Noma was too small for the truck driver to see him.

Should we have taken our time eating? Should we have left when we were told there were no bungeoppang left? Why were there none left? If there had been bungeoppang, the accident wouldn't have happened. Should we have never given him the bike? Should we have never taught him how to ride the bike? What should we have done? Why did Noma die when he didn't have to, when he was too young to, when it made more sense for him to live? I asked these questions for a long time. I watched him die before me, and I demanded an answer beyond the indifferent logic of a pitch-black night, an icy road with no shoulder or pavement and a tired truck driver barrelling down it at 80 kph. An answer for why the truck materialised when it did, why we were telling dumb jokes, why Noma got on the bike.

Why Noma?

Why did he have to die?

Only a god could answer my questions.

Have they found each other? Is Gu feasting his eyes on Noma's 'sexy' doodles? Are they snickering without me? If we can all be together again in the beyond, I'm ready. Last year, Gu wanted to move somewhere in the mountains, somewhere free from cops and CCTV. *If we live in one of those cabins charred by lightning, high up above like the red squirrels, nobody will realise we're human.* What is it to be human? I had tried so hard, for so long, to be seen as human. Gu seemed to have abandoned the idea altogether. Maybe it was easier, to be an old tree or a red squirrel. So I said, *Sure. Why bother with being human? Let's be animals. Let's be anything but.*

Back then, we were living out of a tiny motel in a satellite village and doing odd jobs that didn't ask for CVs or ID. Our earnings went straight into a wallet the size of my palm. It lived with me because Gu could be plucked off the street at any minute. In his pocket, he carried a fist as hard as a rock. The many years of manual labour had sculpted his arms to perfection, like a finely sharpened pencil. I almost went crazy tearing into them, those arms that had held and guided me. I slapped myself. To keep alert. To see what I was eating. To never forget.

After Noma, we went our separate ways for a time.

And even when our paths crossed, our eyes barely met. It was impossible to laugh, cry, speak. In our hearts was a chasm too big to look at, let alone fill.

We couldn't do it.

They say that you should stick together through the hard times, but we couldn't do it. Noma died right before our eyes. That wasn't a 'tough time'. It was beyond language.

—How hard this must be on Gu.

Auntie urged me to reach out.

—Who but you can understand what he's going through?

I realised that was exactly why I couldn't. I saw both myself and Noma in Gu, and I imagined he saw the same. I didn't want to see him in pain, and I didn't want to become his pain.

Time apart will do us good, I thought. Time for the accident to dim from my eyes, for the replay to end. After a time, I would be back at my station at the factory gates and searching for the North Star. I mean, me and Gu. We were meant to be.

I had accepted the fact as a kid. *You and I will be together until the day we die. And even when we're not, we'll be together.* Our childhoods were lived together – hearing, seeing, feeling the same things. Bad things, good things, embarrassing things – everything, together. Over the years, our hearts grew to echo together even when we weren't.

Gu and I were once separate entities.

Then one day, a droplet of emotion fell and swelled until it became big enough to bridge the chasm between us. It made us complete, like cartilage cushioning bones, like a long-missing puzzle piece clicking perfectly into place.

You and I will be together until the day we die.

And even when we're not, we'll be together.

What do they call this feeling? It was bigger than 'love', but love was the closest thing to it. It clung to our skin and spirits, surviving us even in death.

I waited a long time in this certainty.

Then I waited some more, reciting Auntie's mantra.

Everything passes.

Just let it pass.

As long became longer, I lost track of what I was waiting to pass.

Was it time? Or Gu?

Jinju had a way of treating me like a younger brother.

—What's a kid like you doing in a job like this? Don't your parents give you an allowance? Are you saving up for uni or something? When do you find the time to study? Do you even have the grades to get in? All right, all right, eat up. Eat before you go. Leftovers, from the funeral. Everyone else is eating, look. You shouldn't sleep on an empty stomach. Get some meat on those bones. Do you know how many people pass out around here? Hey, want some booze? You can hold your drink, right?

She set down a plate of braised pig's feet and kimchi on a plastic crate before dragging over another to sit on. I really didn't want to talk to her, not even to decline her offer. After Noma, I gave up speaking unless strictly necessary and people generally left me be. Except Jinju. She wouldn't be stopped, pressuring me to eat.

—Hey kid, stop acting like some old sage who's seen it all. How are your grades? What's your ranking? Or have you given up on school? That's not the answer either, is it? Kid, you should aim for community college at the very least. Or vocational school. Oh sit down, will you. I'm looking out for you. You got anyone else to give you advice? Your parents are too busy looking out for themselves. That's why a kid like you is working here when you should be studying. Go on, tell me I'm wrong.

Jinju's lectures always came with a side of food. Kimbap. Hamburgers. Milk. Steamed buns. Mandu. Rice balls. Sikhye. Red ginseng extract. Onion juice. In the beginning, I wouldn't touch any of it. Then she started leaving snacks on top of my jacket and backpack. I ended up scarfing them down, barely chewing before swallowing and heading out. I couldn't throw away perfectly good food, could I?

—If you're going to eat it anyway, you might as well enjoy it hot.

I ate everything without a word as she talked my ear off. Eventually, Jinju became a habit. I ended up eating her stew every night.

—I've been keeping an eye on you, you know.

Jinju handed me a bowl of kimchi stew with cold rice mixed in.

—Ever since the accident, you start crying the second you set foot outside the factory. A kid like you with his face all wet, turning into skin and bones. I don't like it, not one bit.

It had happened. To Noma. A kid. I hated the pity coming my way when he was dead. It was wrong, almost sinful.

—I haven't seen that girl in a while, the one who used to wait for you. How's she doing? I took you for siblings, but you're a couple, aren't you?

I set down my spoon. Jinju handed it back to me without missing a beat.

—Eat your food, eat. I'll stop talking.

I didn't want to think about Dam. I wanted to walk with her, and I was scared to walk with her. I wanted to see her, and I never wanted to see her again. I wouldn't show my feelings, because if I were ever to cry or laugh again, it had to be with Dam. Not this woman.

Jinju kept pestering me, trying to break down my walls.

She was newly thirty and already divorced with a kid her ex-husband had custody of, having lost touch with her parents somewhere along the way. She nursed no big dreams of striking it rich and winning back her son, but she wanted to do her part to help with university, his travels, or a wedding if he ever came up short. Noma reminded her of him, she said. It was the last thing I wanted to hear. I sat there, swallowing my tears as she prised out everything I was holding back with her invasive questions, like *What are you planning to do with your life?*

I spent a long time dodging that one, shoving everything it stirred up right back down. The future was too much. My mind tripped and fell into a grave of debt whenever it tried to map out the way. My muscles for the future were slack and powerless. My future felt like a flat, lukewarm and non-alcoholic beer. I kept sneaking the cap back on, trying to convince everyone it was as good as new. *It scares me how life is passing me by*, I confessed a long time ago. Dam had reassured me it would all be okay, but she was also holding back. Lovers are always holding something back. The truth is bitter, but someone has to swallow it.

—My parents are drowning in debt and clutching at straws trying to pay up, but we keep sinking deeper and deeper.

Jinju asked how it all started.

—I don't know. I woke up and I was in debt.

I had never told anyone but Dam.

A less clichéd answer sat on the tip of my tongue. Jinju just happened to be there. Or maybe she set it loose. I was sick and tired of holding back.

—What the hell would I know? I'm out here working my fingers to the bone, but we don't live in a world that rewards hard work, do we? I guess you haven't figured that one out, have you?

I yelled at a thirty-year-old woman who seemed hardly any more mature than me.

My classmates were busy applying to university, sold on the popular belief that school is only a stepping stone to a degree. I had no such ambitions. My aunt agreed university was probably a good idea, but given my mediocre grades, teachers weren't interested in my future. The choice was mine, but it felt like an impossible one to make. And it wasn't much of a choice. If I went, I'd spend two to four years working for one employer to pay for the various qualifications demanded by another employer. And would that even be enough to guarantee me a spot at a top company? The things that were supposedly normal twenty-something things – networking, landing internships, studying abroad, going for a PhD – read like science fiction. Every conversation about university circled back to the job market. My classmates were obsessed with getting rich quick and achieving financial freedom. I was continually reminded, even by people my age, that I had no idea how the world worked. 'No, that's not true,' 'Not a chance,' or 'Easier said than done.' These catchphrases punctuated their sentences and punctured my skull, plunging me into a depression. I hadn't even got started, and failure was already guaranteed. Life had won.

I guess listening to them map out the future helped me forget, for a bit.

But unhappiness found me.

It was strange how it sneaked in, even as the memory of Noma's death dimmed.

And stranger still was how it found a way through the distance from Gu.

My thoughts often drifted to Auntie. *Why should she keep working to prove her love for me? When will she be allowed to rest?* I was her burden, all because my future required money.

—It must be tough, working all the time.

—That's life.

—I'm sorry.

—Why the sudden apology?

—Auntie, I'm thinking of going into nursing. I heard you can get rich quick.

—If by 'quick' you mean four years.

—Right. Should I not go to uni, then?

—Whether you go or not, I'll still have to work at least another two decades.

—Why's that?

—What else would I do? Just sit around all day?

—You could do something easier on your body.

—There's no such thing as an easy job.

—I'm sorry.

—What for?

—I make things harder on you.

—Dam?

—Yeah?

—I'm blessed to have you in my life. A lady of my age without parents, husband or kids.

—When I start earning, Auntie, I'll treat you. I will.

—You'll buy me a trip to South East Asia?

—Yes.

—And Jeju Island?

—Of course.

—And hiking clothes?

—Done.

She exhaled.

—Gu better not get saddled with debt. I haven't a clue how he'll manage.

I said nothing.

—You worry about him, don't you?

I said nothing.

—That's important. Never forget how you feel about him.

—Worried?

—Yes, sweetheart. Worry is what keeps us from making the world uglier.

—Well, I'm full of worry. I worry about you, about Gu, about myself, about our futures. I'm made of worry, and the world looks ugly.

—Dam?

—Yes?

—I do the worrying about you.

She gently touched my shoulder.

68

—Let's eat. I sure hope that guy's taking care of himself and going to work on a full stomach.

—What if he isn't eating at all?

—We've all got to eat, don't we?

My heart hurt. What if he was waiting for me? I wanted to make sure he was healthy, at the very least. My worry for him swelled, eclipsing my worry for myself, just as one tragedy eclipses another.

Jinju's room was small, warm and on the second floor of an apartment building. She'd serve me kimchi or pollack stew with a bottle of soju, preferring to drink from her own bottle. The room had no TV or radio. The silence was almost total at night, except for a couple arguing or a neighbour singing at the top of their lungs every now and then. A short while after my visits became routine, I'd hear a motorcycle rumbling down the alley around 2.30am. I figured it was either a food or newspaper delivery guy. As he drew closer, I heard the song. The man had an impressive voice. It didn't sound like any song I knew.

—Always the same song. Every night, like clockwork, the motorcycle rolls in with that tune. I know every note by heart. I don't know him or his face, but when a night goes by without the song, I worry. And when it comes back, I feel a strange relief.

She murmured more to herself than anyone else.

—He probably doesn't have a clue there's a woman out there he's never met who worries about him every day.

*

More and more, I found myself heading straight to work after a late night of drinking with Jinju. In the beginning, I'd leave right after finishing off my soju without lingering at her door. I always tried to make it home, but stumbling back drunk and exhausted one night, I saw the light on in my parents' room. The house was usually pitch-black at that hour. I really didn't want to go inside.

After getting a job, my father occasionally offered me soju. I never took it because accepting his soju would have been like agreeing to take on his burden with a handshake, like saying *I understand you.* I'd never openly disobeyed my parents, never voiced my regrets or complaints. If work needed doing, I did it. If money needed earning, I earned it. Accountability wasn't on the menu. I knew better than anyone my parents didn't have it easy, but I didn't understand them. I wouldn't shake hands with him, guzzling his soju in exchange for a look of sympathy. When it came to my parents, my best was somewhere between bitterness and forgiveness.

I stood at the front door looking up at the light, before turning on my heels and walking back to Jinju's. That night, I had sex with her for the first time. It was fine. We undressed like we drank soju – separately. She was face up, spreading her legs. I took a quick look before inserting myself. I thrust, squeezed her breasts a few times, and came quickly. Then I was out like a light. I woke up in the middle of the night, but it was time to get ready for work. Jinju had prepared some soybean soup for dinner, which she now mixed with an egg yolk and served on cold rice. I took it, chewed slowly, and left. It was the first time I'd had hot soup before work. It comforted and crushed me.

I regularly asked myself why Jinju hit on me, fed me, listened to me, took me in, shared her bed. I tried seeing the situation from her perspective. According to her, she found me irritating and wanted to give me a piece of her mind. I knew that wasn't the truth. Jinju was kind, bubbly and petite, and quite a few guys at work had a crush on her. The supervisor tried setting her up on dates, some of which she went on. So why was I doing it? Going over every night to eat her food and put my dick in her, insisting she suck me off and whine like a child for a bath? I never liked home to begin with, but after discovering her room, I hated it. Jinju intensified my anger at the world. I eventually realised I would never understand her without understanding myself.

My heart . . . Dam understood it. All of it. She got me on every level, always putting a name to my feelings. My heart sank thinking of her, like the dam holding back my emotions had burst. I wondered if she could sense that there was another woman. Had Jinju forced her way into my heart? Dam knew all about my family, my friends, my past, my darkness, Noma. And that's exactly why I couldn't see her. With Dam, I never asked myself who made the first move because there was no room for 'why' between us. With Jinju, I interrogated the void, *Why the hell us?* Jinju believed relationships between men and women are all about timing. Yes, we were a man, a woman, and our relationship better fit the definition, leaving me even more puzzled. If our arrangement required a rationale, would it be termed love?

Thinking about Dam hurt. Facing my parents hurt. Thinking about the future hurt. In my hurt, I found Jinju. I'd go to her room knowing I shouldn't, and I'd leave promising myself I wouldn't. And the days piled up, one on top of the other.

I couldn't bring myself to use a knife or hold a flame to his flesh. It was him, even in death. His body became pale and stiff like an old rice cake, but it was still the body that had once felt every one of my touches, licks, leans, sucks. *What is beauty?* I asked. Gu's body was skinny and scrawny and beautiful. Our life together had not always been beautiful, and beautiful moments had made a home in our imperfection. I wanted to be the only person who knew everything there was to know about Gu. The idea of him feeling something I couldn't understand, of not occupying his thoughts for a single second, was unbearable and simply unacceptable. I needed to be there, in his joy and pleasure, sorrow and despair. My only desire was Gu. *No one will remember us, Dam. We will remember ourselves*, he said a long time ago, disposable camera in hand. The first time we took a photo together, we were twenty-three. I carried it with me everywhere like a talisman. I had someone, someone who remembered me, remembered us. Back then, we felt so much lighter because we were together. Our emotions coloured in one shade, our gazes trained in the same direction.

Every night, the musk of chestnut blossoms on our skin intoxicated us.

I couldn't do it. I couldn't let his body spoil. I would bury him inside me, every last morsel. I tore through his skin as a thousand regrets raced through my mind. I wondered if burning him or scattering his ashes in the sea would have been more merciful . . . but there was no going back now. I had chosen, and no law, no gun, no god could stop me now. Only him. Only Gu held the power to stop me. If he appeared in a dream and said something, whether to stop, continue, or even if he just looked at me, anything would change everything. The world will call me a crazy bitch, a psychopath, inhuman, but what does he think of me? It's his body, isn't it? Criticise me, imprison me, execute me. I couldn't care less. So long as I can eat all of Gu. So long as I can give him this funeral.

In Jinju's room, I heard the rain close the curtain on spring, endured the oppressive heat of midsummer and caught the first cricket song of the season.

In Jinju's room, I killed over fifty mosquitoes and went through more than three hundred eggs and twenty boxes of soju. Every weekend, I helped clean up. I changed fluorescent light bulbs, fixed the tap, deep-cleaned the stove and assembled a shoe rack. I bought a pot of yellow flowers and killed them within a month. I never walked to the market with her. Jinju avoided being seen with me in public, worried about the gossip that would spread if the factory workers caught on.

When we got wasted, things started off cute and soon turned vicious as all our bottled-up frustration got unleashed on the nearest target. The things we put up with sober sneaked under our skin. It was like playing ping-pong instead of catch. Jinju's rejections and objections seemed to come from the whole world. When she'd start lecturing me about life and death, I'd lose it and storm out. I had heard it all before and resolved to ignore her, particularly the painfully clichéd sayings about money fixing everything that made me feel like a broke loser without a clue about the world. *I'm saying it for your own good*, she'd say patronisingly. I know she was coming from a place of concern, but it was like she was telling me to fuck off and die, like there was no hope left for me. Back then, I couldn't take people at face value. The next day, with all the insults hurled and the fights fought, we would continue dipping our spoons into the same pot of spicy stew like nothing happened.

Eventually, Jinju gave up bombarding me with questions and began talking about herself. How she met her ex-husband, why they divorced. Her clever, silly son. What her parents were like. Then she regaled me with tales from her teenage years: her friends, her fifteenth birthday, her school field trip, the boy she liked, the boy who liked her, the awkwardness of her first relationship and break-up, her twentieth birthday, the debauchery of university. Her storytelling was all over the place. I listened passively, periodically nodding or throwing her a 'Really?' It upset her so much she'd fly into a rage mid-story. *Aren't you even a little curious? Don't you feel anything for me? Not sad or jealous? Not even pity? Nothing, huh?*

Her questions annoyed me because I couldn't answer them. No, I wasn't curious or jealous. Yes, I felt nothing. Yet I couldn't bring myself to say the words that would shatter anyone's heart. I didn't want to hurt her.

I thought of Dam every single day.

She wouldn't tell me about the past because we'd lived it

together. If she brought up the time when we were eleven, catching summer minnows in a brook, I could chime in and finish off the story. *As in the time we almost died because you dropped your shoe in the water? That time?* Our conversations flowed with emotion, without any need for explanation. The silences were never awkward or uncomfortable. When Jinju told me about the time she almost got kicked out on her fifteenth birthday because the neighbour caught her in the playground with a boy, drunk out of her mind, it took me back to making birthday pancakes with Dam, our first sips of beer and the days spent playing house under the slide. The past meant everything to me. I looked at Jinju. It was as if thirty years had flashed by. As if no matter how many mountains I scaled, no matter how many rivers I crossed, I would never find a way back to Dam.

◯

The day was stifling, as if the world were simmering in a cooker. People stuck together like grains of rice, finding it impossible to stand each other. Even after the punishing sun had dipped behind the mountains, the heat lingered. After getting back late from school, I was too exhausted to change and collapsed onto the floor in my uniform. The few nutrients remaining in my body had finally been sapped. It hit me that summer could be as brutal as winter. I dozed off, only to be wakened in the pitch-dark by the sound of rain pouring, even though there had been no hint of a storm earlier. I looked up at the clock, which periodically stopped working. Gu had changed the batteries twice. Auntie and I always ended up checking another clock, moving from clock to clock until every single one in the house had met the same fate. Then, we were left with guesswork. Gu made that clock tick again.

I grabbed two umbrellas and stepped outside.

Six months had passed. I was about to see Gu for the first time in half a year.

Winter had gone, and I couldn't remember if spring had come. And now, summer was halfway over.

The downpour was torrential. Even armed with an umbrella, I ended up thoroughly soaked. I knew it would soon catch up with me; summer colds always followed storms like this. Back in the day, Gu and I used to fall ill together. Auntie would bring us medicine to share.

I called out to Gu when he exited the factory, but the rain swallowed my voice. He had no umbrella, only a backpack to shield his head. As he crossed the road, the distant headlights of a speeding car made my heart race before he safely made it to the other side. A woman emerged from a narrow alley.

And that's when I saw it.

Gu and the other woman, strolling together under an umbrella the size of a parasol and leaving the factory behind. He pulled her close, his arm wrapped protectively around her shoulders. The pair ran across the road, their footsteps in sync. I watched them drift apart and come together as they sailed through puddles in the winding alleys, his arm never once leaving her shoulder. He might as well have carried her. I watched their shadows dissolve into the street lamp's glow before disappearing into the same house. A moment later, the second-storey window lit up. I stared for a small eternity at the frosted glass shut tight. My body trembled like a twig in a winter storm, struggling to keep the umbrella steady. I eventually succeeded in peeling my eyes away. An overflowing bin bag stood beneath the street lamp, somehow untouched by the heavy rains. The pounding of my heart joined the clamour of rain, wind and traffic in a single, unrelenting chorus.

You and I will always be together.
Even when we're not, we'll be together.

A noise spilled out of the bin bag. I knelt before it, trying to undo the knot which was as tight as pursed lips. I convinced myself the bag contained clues to Gu's new life. I wanted to pull them out. I wanted to know. If I couldn't know his life, I wanted to at least have something of his. And if I couldn't have it, I wanted to throw it all away with my own two hands. The knot remained as stubborn as ever. My umbrella kept slipping from where it was wedged between my shoulder and neck. I wondered if he was watching from the window. I wondered what my face looked like. I grabbed the bin bag and looked up at the window, but I still couldn't make anything out.

—Gu.

I called out to him in a whisper barely audible to myself.

Why are you in there? I wanted to ask, but I was scared of the answer. Two silhouettes flickered behind the frosted window. Silence swallowed me, and everything blurred. Then I saw everything all at once. As if I had reached the mountain peak after wandering lost. My heartbeat slowed and stilled. I set down the bin bag as it finally burst, splattering my feet.

I got home drenched and peeled off my school uniform before tossing it on the drying rack and jumping in the shower. A cold was inevitable. My head throbbed, my muscles ached. I almost wanted to be ill to the point of delirium, like a light bulb filament ready to snap. Will he catch a cold? Will he get sick with me this summer? Will he? Oh right, the umbrella. I'd lost the umbrella I'd brought for Gu. Where had I dropped it? If the rain beat on into the morning, I'd skip school with or without a cold. Auntie slowly rose from her sleep, like a shadow lifting from the floor to the wall. She wrung out my uniform skirt before neatly hanging it on the drying rack.

—You're going to catch a cold.

—Yep.

—It's chucking it down. What were you doing out so late?

—Auntie, don't you ever go on dates?

She snorted. I continued.

—Wouldn't it be nice if you had a boyfriend over on a wet summer day? We'd make pajeon, drink a bit of soju. We'd have fun. When will we? I have to learn how to drink from you adults.

—How long until your university entrance exams?

—I don't know, a hundred days? If you date, I'll get you an anniversary present.

We fell into silence.

—Dam?

—Yeah?

—I . . . do just fine for myself.

—You do?

—I go out when I can.

—Come on, be serious.

She laughed. Then, with a more serious expression, she

gestured to the shelf beside the fridge. There it was: her famous plum wine.

—I'll teach you how to drink. Let's polish it off this winter.

—No, I don't want to drink with you alone. Come on, bring home a man already!

I turned my back to her. Every summer, Auntie would prepare around six bottles of maesil-ju. Every winter, she'd scoop out the plums, mark the bottling date and savour the wine from two years past. Sometimes, she'd pour me a couple of glasses to ease my period cramps. A drink and a nap later, the pain would be gone. I assumed the alcohol had worked its magic, but she put it down to the plums. Arguably, I had picked up a drinking habit from my aunt. Alcohol was my painkiller. What was it to Auntie? What did that plum wine mean to my aunt?

—Auntie?

She said nothing.

—I want to drink.

She returned soft snores. Again, I turned over to face her.

—Everyone dates, so why don't you?

The storm raged on. I wanted to say something, anything, but the words wouldn't come. Maybe I didn't want to speak. Maybe I just needed to cry. I didn't want to wake Auntie with my sobs, and I didn't want to watch her sleep soundly through my tears.

The crying would have to wait.

Once the rain stops, I'll go to Gu again. No. First, I'll catch a cold, drink maesil-ju and get healthy. Then I'll go. And after, I'll cry. After gazing into his eyes, holding his hand and feeling its grip.

In the winter days leading to my graduation, I was still patrolling the market, the factory and the two convenience stores. I practically lived at the factory during the holidays. I already knew how to drive and planned on getting the licence to prove it. Driving a truck meant big money. And I dreamed of driving her to the sea. I never talked much about Dam with Jinju. To her, Dam was no more than an ex to envy. I guess she eventually sensed there was more to the story, something that ran deeper and truer than my money problems. It wasn't my predicament or my future that pushed her away; it was that impenetrable 'something' that finally made her give up.

In those days, I noticed a man trying to win Jinju. He dropped by the factory monthly to inspect the goods and place orders. Jinju would sort the ledgers for him, serve him tea and arrange a full-course meal at the Chinese restaurant in the city centre. The man appeared to be in his late thirties, having hit all the expected milestones: a degree, a good job, a small villa bought with savings, and a car loan. There was only one item left on his to-do list – marriage.

A few other guys had shown interest in Jinju, but she always spoke about them with a casual indifference. She had come to believe that, at her age, dating is a calculation: you meet, size each other up and see if they're worth your time. *After a while, you start feeling and treating others like a product.* You skip the talking stage and go straight to the bottom line. *It's different with you. You're like a real, living, breathing person with a heart that hasn't shrivelled up*, she said.

And that's what had exhausted her. Jinju was easily irritated and complained about being sick of it all, insisting on handling things herself. I was to mind my own business. Then her eyes would well up with concern and pity, but she didn't know if she was crying for me or for herself. The confusion led her to nag and meddle until she finally saw things for what they were.

Because she had worn her heart out.

Because she had given her all.

Because she no longer saw me as a real, living, breathing person.

Jinju suggested we go our separate ways in the spring.

—You're still young, and I'm not exactly dead. It's better we split before it's too late. You've got to leave this place and start again. Now that school's out, get yourself to a city. The further, the better. Cut off your parents. Choose a trade. Save up some cash and spend it all on yourself. You've got time to do things right.

It wasn't the dumping that hurt but the so-called advice that followed. She was basically telling me to get lost. She didn't want to be with me or be there for me, choosing to turn us into strangers forever. I was furious at her for parading that as advice.

—Tell me something I don't know! I know all that, and I can't fucking deal with it. Knowing doesn't make things easier! Can you stop pretending everything is so simple?

I lashed out, acting like someone who'd lost everything in a blink, like someone who saw something valuable snatched out of their hands. Jinju's words had unleashed all my pent-up feelings, exposing just how fiercely my heart was roaring inside. Is life easier without knowing? Is it even helpful to understand and express the emotions that govern you? Inside me were a host of clashing personalities vying for supremacy: a tyrant, a bitter child, a scared boy, a heartless soul, a sex maniac. Anxiety gushed through my veins like a poison, burning my throat with frustration and laughter. I needed, yearned to be loved. Deeply.

I joined the army. I decided not to tell anyone – not my parents, not Dam, not Jinju, not my co-workers. I wanted to vanish from everywhere I'd ever set foot and find someplace nobody knew me. I wanted a perfect solitude, a shot at change. And if I couldn't change, I would throw myself away and start from scratch.

○

My aunt and grandfather spent more years apart than together. They were very different people. For Grandpa, a good meal consisted of alcohol with meat on the side; Auntie only indulged in meat on special occasions. He ate simply but feasted at dinner; Auntie snacked throughout the day. He loved the ladies; she loved the Buddha. Grandpa worried where Auntie radiated calm. His mantra: 'That's just the way life goes.' Hers: 'This too shall pass.' I wonder if they were getting at the same thing.

My aunt died from the same illness that took grandfather.

Once diagnosed, it advanced rapidly like it had been lying in wait to be called by name. Auntie knew she would meet a sudden end like her father. She had no final words for me – what she knew, I knew, and what I didn't know, she didn't either. After she got diagnosed, she would start and end every one of our conversations with 'I love you'. I'd estimate she said those words over a thousand times. I've heard 'I love you' more than anyone else in the world. The day of her final breath, she mouthed for me to take care of myself. I couldn't say goodbye.

As her body was fed into the cremator, I was struck by the horror of her dissolving into ash. After everything life had thrown at her, it seemed cruel to consign her to the flames. If I could, I would have stayed by her side. So what if her soul was gone? Her body wasn't. I believed that so long as her body remained, she could still hear, see, feel.

Life, you win. I lost. I'm a loser . . . I muttered to myself throughout the cremation. A hazy childhood memory flashed in my mind: my grandfather's hunched back against the blue of dawn, his silhouette a perfect black. The colours of loneliness. One day, I saw my sick aunt hunched over. I wept in my sleep. The truth that she, too, would pass rang out from inside me. Auntie was unfazed by my outburst, simply rubbing my back and whispering softly.

—It's okay, baby, it'll pass. Everything passes.

But is that true, Auntie?

Some things don't pass. They settle and fester.

After the three days of mourning, I lay flat on the floor with every light in the house on like a kid scared of ghosts. I replayed the last look she gave me, over and over again.

Grandpa, Auntie, and now even Gu are gone. I am alone in this life.

Every day, I consider the meaning of that sentence.

○

I am alone in this life.

Meaning, I am alone in this body.

The day we went on the run, Gu and I visited Auntie and Grandpa. We laid their memorial tablets to rest at the temple where my aunt had lived before becoming Auntie. It was a simple place nestled in the mountains like a smooth apple seed, a cold wind sweeping through it carrying snow. Gu made a deep, long bow before the tablets. An elderly nun recognised me and took my hand, asking after my well-being and gently stroking my back like Auntie used to. She asked us to stay for mealtime, and I agreed. Then she asked us to stay for a night or two. I turned to Gu, his face soft like a sleeping cat. Gu asked if I came here often. I used to visit with her every now and then, but after she died, the idea of coming alone terrified me. It would've made it too real, as if giving in to death. I missed and spoke to her every day, waiting for a reply that seemed like it might come from wherever she'd gone. It was my only comfort. Back when I'd visited the temple with my aunt, I noticed a stack of roof tiles inscribed with wishes:

'Pass exams' 'Business success'

'Longevity' 'Family health'

'True love'

—Do you think the Buddha will grant these? I doubt it. It's the sort of wish that doesn't really align with his teachings. He'd grant other things.

—Such as?

—Uh, world peace?

Auntie roared. The roof tiles from back in the day were still piled high by the temple's office. I asked Gu what he wished for. After thinking, he spoke.

—To be freed from this suffering.

He hesitated for a moment before adding.

—And if that's not doable, then let this lifetime fly by.

—But that means you'll die sooner. I can't let that happen.

—Then let me be nothing again, nothing and everything.

—That's dying.

—It's not. It's courage.

My heart echoes his wish, but the meanings of life, pain and courage cloud and scatter. The wind howls, threatening to tear the door off its hinges. I haven't seen my own face in a while. I ended up smashing every reflective surface on a random night. Gu wouldn't approve of what this place has become, our mess of blankets in this creepy room. I probably look like a bedraggled wildcat that's barely survived a tussle with a boar.

I look like crap, don't I?

I'm begging for a sign, even a bad one.

I'm still here, alive and kicking. The house is unimaginably cold. Outer space can reach temperatures below -270 degrees Celsius. You wouldn't rot. You'd stay pretty, like a sailboat gliding through the cosmos in a glass bottle. I wouldn't have to know the taste of your flesh. If only we could be boats, sinking into that bottomless blackness of nothing and everything, observing the beautiful galaxy untouched by human concerns. If only it were a billion years in the future, I'd leave Earth with your body on my back and we'd be a pair of happy boats. Doesn't that sound nicer than cannibalism? I open the front door and observe the countless stars, like pallid carcasses frozen in light. Will we exist in a billion years, in that faraway place without air, light or sound?

Is it very cold where you are?

I sit very still, waiting for him to answer.

No calls or letters found me. To be fair, I hadn't reached out to anyone. I debated writing to Dam, and I settled on saying it to her face.

I was the youngest in my unit. I had always been the youngest. The factory, the supermarket, the convenience stores – everywhere except school. I never gave it much thought. I was used to how adults spoke and saw the world, growing to feel more comfortable around them than those my own age. Back at school, I was invisible. It took several back-to-back absences for people to notice. Even when my form teacher came to deliver a final warning at the factory, I don't think he really saw me as a student. *When will you get your life together?* the adults kept asking. I was felling trees in the army when I realised: a seventeen-year-old is too young to answer that sort of question.

A regimented life. A job taken on for something other than money. Matching clothes, hairstyles, words. Days free from drinking and women. In the barracks, I discovered health and camaraderie. The guys were in it together – working, eating, sleeping side by side. The best part was that money had no power in the army. Without it hanging over my head, I could think straight.

The night before my first leave, I hardly slept. I was determined to see her, but my excitement faded and my worry intensified as the day dawned. What if she hated me? What if she didn't even live there anymore? The idea of seeing her terrified me, and the idea of not seeing her terrified me. I knew I had to see her. I knew I couldn't put it off any longer.

I realised the army was my safe space on the first day of leave. The world outside the barracks was pretty much the same. My parents had been booted out, now relegated to an even smaller room at the back of their shop. The dust on every surface was piled so high one sneeze would send a cloud blooming through the air, shrouding my mother's hair and shoulders. I never once saw my father's face during my leave. *Dam's aunt died. She lasted six months after her diagnosis*, my mother announced. And, in that moment, my worries, anxieties, all became trivial in the face of Dam. Alone with death. I'd run off to the army, abandoning her to get high on health and fake confidence. *I missed you. I was thinking of you.* I wanted to tell her but that would have been even more irresponsible. The urge rose again, to run away and silently uproot trees, to level the ground at the base. I wanted to run laps around the parade ground, armed to the teeth, until I collapsed in an exhausted heap. I wanted to crawl around and get stepped on.

*

The last day of leave, I saw her. In the distance, for a moment. She was thinner and smaller but somehow sturdier, like a cold, dry stone. I struggled to even look, never mind speak to her. The sorrow she radiated reached me through the distance. I couldn't believe it. Auntie was dead. The only person who'd ever slipped me an allowance, who looked out for me. I watched Noma die, right before me. But Auntie? It was like she was still out there, somewhere, like she'd just moved to a new home. I got on the bus back to the base without saying a word to Dam, saying goodbye to Auntie or sorting any of my problems out. I was losing Dam for good. The realisation hit me harder than the break-up with Jinju or joining the military, and I broke down. This was an agonising grief with no match.

○

I had no family, no friends, no Gu, no one to look out for me.
I took a job at a grocery store in the city centre, selling sirloin
and tenderloin, pork shoulder and belly, ham. I was lucky to
get that job, what with everything else in town being taken.
The other kids either ventured off to college or big cities
where most ended up in retail, putting up with customers.
Meanwhile, I sliced meat in silence. The boss applauded me
for taking such good care of the knives. I liked the knives. The
weight of one in my hand made me feel safe. I liked the ritual
of washing a sharp blade and patting it dry with a dishcloth
before gliding it through tendon. I also liked Mendelssohn.
Back when she worked at the factory, Auntie passed the hours
listening to the radio on an old MP3 player. The first time I
turned it on, classical music flowed out and filled the air. I
forgot the German title instantly, but that player became my
greatest treasure. With my earbuds in, I felt a little less alone.
The market, forever pulsing with the blare of pounding
music and inane radio presenters, assaulted my senses. In the
lulls, I'd escape to my nook behind the freezer and tune into
her favourite station. I pretended it was really hers, as if she

95

herself was playing the music especially for me. I appreciated how music didn't ask me to laugh or cry. The ritual became like a prayer whispered before falling asleep, a lifeline when the world left me no way out. Gripping my first pay packet, I headed straight for the back of the local record store where the Mendelssohn CDs lay clothed in dust. I chose the one with the best cover, a gift to myself. Actually, let's call it a gift from my aunt in heaven. I also bought a knife and a whetstone that day. Every night, I would whet my knife to the melodies of a string quartet before climbing into bed. My days were mind-numbing: 'Welcome,' 'What can I get you?' 'Is this enough?' 'Thank you,' 'Have a nice day.' There was nothing more to say. I lived the same day again and again, waiting for him. Gu, the only one I wanted to see. It beat waiting for parents and siblings who never turned up when my grandfather and aunt died, who might not even exist. I decided they didn't. It was easier to tell myself they didn't exist. My greatest blessing, Auntie, must have used up all my luck. I guess it was too good to last, but doesn't everything come in pairs? Everything has a counterpart, from the largest star to the smallest atom, meaning she couldn't have been my only luck. There had to be something else. A force that brought her into my life and took her away. I decided that force was him. Gu was coming back. He was coming back because of me. I arrived at the same conclusion every night, sharpening my knife and listening to my aunt's radio station.

●

After that first leave, I stopped going home. I boarded a bus to either coast, staring at the ocean before finding an inn to crash at. My unit leader took a liking to me. The man was three years older and had been studying sociology before enlisting. I told him everything. He just listened, handing me a cigarette without saying a word. After that day, he'd give me ₩30,000 every time I went on leave. *Treat yourself to a nice meal. Rent someplace clean with hot water.* I was made a sergeant when he got discharged, slipping me a packet of cigarettes and ₩50,000 on his way out. I cried. *Call me when you get out. Talk when things get hard. I'm here for you.* I wasn't going to call him, I decided. I refused to be even more indebted to him. I spent about three months as the highest-ranking man in our unit. It was an awkward time. Being in charge. Everyone looking at me. My discharge. I needed to get my head straight, figure out what to do, how to live back in the real world, but nothing solid came to mind. *I'll just work hard and live well. Something will turn up.* I ended up giving myself the pep talk no one else would.

*

After being discharged, I went back to my neighbourhood supermarket and asked for brisket and sirloin. My parents' shop was a mess. The fridge was plugged in, but it didn't work. The electricity and water had been cut off. I tossed the beef into the kitchen and then, worried the rats might claim it, placed it in the tepid fridge. I paced around in a circle, caught between the need to know what had happened and my fear of finding out. I left the shop, sirloin in hand.

Dam.

The reason I came back.

I had to see Dam.

It was late. I heard footsteps approaching, slowly and deliberately, from the bottom of the alley. I stood up slowly from my seat against the wall. I wanted to call her name, but my mouth wouldn't cooperate. I clutched the plastic bag of meat, twirling and fiddling with it before passing it to my other hand. The footsteps stopped, leaving the rustling of the bag to fill the alley.

—. . . You're here.

After a long time, Dam spoke first.

—Have you eaten?

Like we'd seen each other just yesterday.

—What's that?

She gestured at the black bag swinging aimlessly from my wrist.

—Beef.

My first utterance to her in nearly three years.

—Come on. Let's make soup.

She held the door open for me.

—It's actually sirloin. Steak.

My second utterance to her in nearly three years.

—Cool. Let's grill it.

I stood there frozen, staring at her face like an idiot. Dam took my hand. The plastic bag hanging from my wrist still swaying, as if on a stormy sea. My hand, clasped in hers, throbbed with shame.

I knew he would come back.

I had predicted he would come back after being discharged, but it was seeing him there, standing in front of the house, that turned something hard inside me. I swallowed it back down, my tongue and throat crying out in pain. I realised what was hiding beneath my yearning: resentment. I didn't resent anyone other than him. It was only when I saw him that it could finally happen.

Auntie, please don't go. She was walking away. *I'm saying goodbye for now, but don't go far. Leave slowly. Look back often. You know how crap everything is in this place. Never forget me. Since you're doing the leaving first, I'll be the one forgetting first. That's only fair, right?*

Beneath the glow of the street light appeared a younger Auntie, smiling at me. *It's not for me to forget,* she mouthed. *I'll do the worrying about you two.*

And then Gu appeared, watching me intently with his back to her. The scene unfolded like a dream, save for the black plastic bag in his hand spinning us back into reality.

*

We grilled the beef and shared a bottle of maesil-ju dated before my aunt got sick, reminiscing about the old days before she died, before Noma. The days we were as young as Noma. Our laughter punctuated a night of gossiping about our ex-classmates: who had gone to university, who was studying for the civil service exam, who was retaking said exam, who was working in the family store. One had vanished without a trace, and one was working part-time at a fast-food joint. Gu told me about his unit's sergeant. I talked a bit about my co-workers at the butchers, but soon enough, the alcohol kicked in and the small talk wore thin. I went in.

—Whatever happened between you and that lady?

—You really haven't dated anyone since?

—So you two were dating, huh? And don't even think about answering that. I'll kill you.

I chuckled at us, bantering like we were still together. Both of us had grown up so fast only to find ourselves alone.

—Come live with me.

The words slipped out.

My parents had gone missing. My father disappeared first, followed by my mother a few months later. I guess the first person to disappear was technically me – but what does any of that matter? I'd say what matters is that my parents vanished without a trace, leaving me to shoulder the debt alone as a legal adult and their guarantor. The interest alone was more than the principal because they'd borrowed from loan sharks, the only people left who would do business with them. Ever since I was young, I'd asked why they continued to take out loans they couldn't afford until it became clear they had no intention of paying them back. They chose to sink deeper and deeper, paying off debt by running up debt. And when it all came crashing down on me, the only words left to say were, *I'm so lost. I don't know what to do.*

They were nowhere to be found, leading me to believe they were long dead. I would never find the bodies, because if their organs hadn't already been carved out and sold off, the corpses would have been disguised for insurance fraud. I'm not exactly sure when it started, this habit of always assuming the worst-case scenario. My parents, the moneylenders, everyone said the words. *All you've got is your body.* A body . . . not a person, not a human. Human as meat, human as object, human as tool. A person's value is proportional to their bank balance. Our society seems to think it's okay to look down on the poor. And when you're constantly broke and beaten down, you start to think money's the only thing that matters. The more you're knocked down, the more you cling to money, hoping it can put you back together. It's messed up, yeah, but that's how it is.

There was nothing those guys couldn't find out. They knew everything. They knew about my discharge. They knew I was the only one left to suck dry. I bet they were thrilled I was young enough to milk for years. It started with a repayment plan that slowly turned into paying them off, even paying them tribute. The number on the ledger never went down, only up. By their calculations, I would be handing over my wages for the rest of my life. I was basically a slave. I had to leave her. It was the right thing to do.

—We can't break up. We're forever. Don't you know that by now?

I had an inkling but she grabbed a red pen and underlined it as the right answer, confirming that it wasn't just me.

—Do you know what Auntie said to me? 'I'm blessed to have you in my life. A lady of my age without parents, husband or kids.'

Dam spoke without shedding a single tear. I wondered how many times she had cried alone for her aunt.

—Do you know what that means?

She looked me dead in the eye. I shook my head.

—I don't either, but I know it's something to be deeply grateful for. A blessing.

A blessing. I savoured the word.

—You know, I have no parents, or siblings, or even an aunt any more. I have you, and I'm grateful for you.

Grateful, huh?

You fool. What do you mean, we can't break up? We'd be better off apart.

Should I have said that? Basically told her to fuck off? Would that have been more loving?

I tried everything. I worked as a mover, builder, driver, valet, living off Dam and using my earnings to pay back the interest. At this rate, I'd be paying off the interest alone until my dying day. I even considered resorting to the law, but the world of money doesn't play by any rule book. My parents, having been scammed repeatedly, eventually looked beyond the law for money. Even if a couple of loan sharks got reported and jailed, the rest of the gang would come to collect their dues. What kept me chained to them wasn't a piece of paper or a promise: it was their brutality, their coercion.

—There's no escaping this. Don't test me.

The second loan shark barked an order at me. I was to hunt down other broke people and extort them through threats, violence, whatever it took to get the job done. I failed. They responded by putting me up in a nightclub, intercepting my pay. I waited tables for a few months before getting transferred to a male host bar. Drinking, singing, kissing, touching – I was to provide everything except sex, not that it didn't happen. The clients took me to after-parties and motels. I fucked them, but they wanted 'the full boyfriend experience'. If I could've kept my tips away from the loan sharks and spoiled Dam with good food, a nice place, no worries about bills and lots of spending money, I would've bent over backwards.

I wasn't making enough at the bar. The loan sharks arranged to ship me overseas and sell me off. Literally.

—Let's run away, Gu.

—Oh, give up already. Before it's too late.

—What do you mean?

—I mean get the fuck off me.

A low, cold voice broke out of me. I looked her dead in the eye with not a hint of remorse showing on my face.

Some are born into war zones, knowing nothing but conflict from their first breath to their last. Some children die starved and diseased. Some die in regions ravaged by epidemics. Some are swept up in wars started by their ancestors, spending their lives as refugees. I believe money can be just as brutal. The debt became a parasite clinging to Gu's life, eating away at his humanity and sucking him dry. It's all the same in the end. The debt was simply the world he inherited, and he had to find a way to survive it. What should we have done? What could we have done?

Are those who fire the guns and take the bullets ever those who start the war?

In early autumn, around Chuseok, a customer came into the shop requesting soup meat. I was busy meticulously slicing and wrapping sirloin for the holiday hampers. I looked up from the cutting board to find an old friend who had encouraged me to join her in nursing school. She had got on to her dream course, but she was now taking a break after one semester because she simply couldn't afford tuition and rent on top of everything else. My friend had planned to become a nurse to make good money, only to find she needed money to make money.

—Turns out life rarely goes according to plan.

She took the meat from me and left.

Gu told me to be happy without him, but I remembered the days without him. The day he faced our bullies, the day Noma died. The days spent waiting to get back together, waiting even after getting back together. If we broke up again, I would spend a lifetime waiting and wondering where he was and what he was doing. I could follow his advice: meet someone good, marry, have their children, buy a house. And be unhappy with a life gained by losing him, every little flaw a reminder of my punishment for leaving him. And every hint of happiness ignored for thoughts of him. He already lived in my mind, when I was happy and when I was sad. I wanted to live with him, not with my thoughts of him.

—We were never any good together. It's just a childish obsession.

He was convinced everything would take a turn for the worse. The more miserable things got, the lonelier our relationship would feel. It would become a torture without relief.

—I wish I could be the guy who makes your life better, but I'm not that guy. I don't think I ever will be.

Gu's voice was ice-cold, but his eyes betrayed the deep terror of an orphan. I fired back.

—It doesn't matter whether you're here or not. I'll be

lonely and unhappy regardless. I'm not saying let's be happy. I'm saying let's be together. I don't mind being unhappy with you.

I wouldn't survive another wait.

—Like if I end up an alcoholic because of you, you should pour me another drink. It's you and me, together. No matter what.

—That's not love.

—I don't care what it is.

I started packing my bags, tossing my aunt's last few belongings into the fire.

○

Noryangjin and Guro, Anyang and Incheon, Busan and Gyeongsan. The first two years were manageable, drifting from place to place and renting small basement rooms. I waited tables. He delivered pizzas. The loan sharks didn't come after us. *Hey, maybe we were just paranoid*, we joked. Then someone showed up at the pizzeria. Gu was out on delivery when his co-worker texted him. He rushed over to my restaurant and we left the city with just the clothes on our backs. Later, he texted back to tell his co-worker where to collect our motorcycle in Seoul. The same thing happened in Incheon and Anyang. The bastards tracked us like the FBI, making it impossible to stay in one place for more than a year. We stopped making friends, stopped calling each other by name. *Is this our punishment?* Our reality filled me with so much rage and fear it broke my spirit.

Then we headed up into the mountains to a small village sandwiched between the Chungcheong, Gangwon and Gyeongsang provinces. I got a job cleaning a luxury motel miles away from anywhere. The boss would ask what a girl like me was doing working at a place like this, and I recited my story: I was paying my way through the college one hour away. I was a public administration student and preparing for the civil service exam. No, I hadn't started studying for it. I had even rehearsed talking about my two siblings with a wistful smile, my dear little brother who was already off to university next year. Yes, our parents were poor – but no one ever asked about any of it. The boss would just call me a 'uni kid' and leave it there. The label seemed to turn me into that aspiring civil servant, missing her older sister and younger brother. Back in the village, the spring trees prospered as the landscape metamorphosed from yellow to white to pink. Then spring gave way to summer. I watched the white buds of the cherry tree flower and fall. Those were quiet, slow days of eating and resting. Gu got his strength back in that room, a haven where we could let our guards down for a while. It was good. I wondered if maybe, just maybe, something good might take root and sprout, even though we were only passing through.

But taking the motel job was a mistake.

The place was like a supermarket, frequented by all kinds of people – drifters, sex workers, gangsters, military men, housewives, teachers, students, truckers, local cops, civil servants, all sorts. One of them spotted Gu. He made a run for it but somehow ended up at the police station, sparking a scuffle between the cops and the loan sharks before escaping in the commotion. Eventually, the loan sharks caught up. Gu was gone for months. I nearly lost it. If he was dead, I wanted to be dead. But if he was dead, I had to find his body and give him a funeral. After one hundred and eighty-five days of agony, he limped back to me.

—Let's go into the mountains and live high up above like the red squirrels.

○

—If you die before me, I will eat you.

It was here, where we had come to become red squirrels, that he said it.

—That's the only way I can live without you, Dam.

I was unfazed by the image of Gu eating me.

—I'd choose dying by your hand over illness or a freak accident.

And there we lay, gazing into each other's eyes and holding every part of each other with every part of our being.

○

—I can't sleep.

I mumbled, pulling him closer. His heart beat slower than mine. I felt each beat against my chest. I could feel it all.

—Wanna hear a story?

He spoke in a whisper.

—Mhmm.

—There once lived a man named Sawney Bean.

—Sorry, what? Sawney . . . Bean?

—It's a name over there.

Gu began.

○

—Sawney Bean and his wife lived in a cave under a sea cliff. They were thieves, lurking by the roads into the village and snatching money, jewels, whatever they could get their hands on. To cover their tracks, they'd kill their victims. But what to do with the bodies, right? After giving it some thought, they settled on eating them.

—The bodies?

—They would chop up the guts and toss them into the sea. Then they would dry and cure the meat, piling the bones high in one corner of the cave. The family kept on robbing, killing and eating people for many years, and, along the way, even had fourteen kids.

—Wow.

—And those fourteen kids grew up on human meat, going on to have twenty-two children of their own.

—In the cave?

—Yep, all in the cave under the sea cliff.

—And they didn't eat each other?

—Nope. They had sex with each other, to grow their numbers. Before long, Sawney Bean's family was up to forty-eight people, running a whole operation. They split up the work – some robbed, others killed, and the rest gutted, dried, cured and stored the meat. They got so good at it that they were making more than they could eat. The rotten meat got tossed out.

—As in they killed more people than they could eat?

—It was just normal to them, like you go to work and trade your earnings for pork at the grocery store.

—So they wouldn't have had any sense of guilt.

—The whole thing went on for twenty-five years until the entire family got arrested and executed. It's said not one of them showed remorse. In fact, they had no idea what they were being arrested for or why people looked horrified. It was simply beyond them because, to their family, killing and eating people wasn't wrong. I wonder if they expected to get eaten by the guards.

I let that sink in.

—And there would have been grandkids too little to do any murdering or stealing themselves, eating whatever the adults gave them to eat, right? It's said even those kids were executed.

—But did those kids know they were eating human flesh?

—They must've.

—And it was probably normal to them?

—I mean, everyone else was doing it.

—Is this a true story?

—It's a Scottish legend. The cave under the sea cliff where the family lived is a tourist hotspot.

—A tourist hotspot . . .

—And even if this one is just an old wives' tale, there

must've been a time in history when people ended up eating other people. Don't you think?

—Probably.

—Maybe even now?

—Probably even now.

—They probably don't feel guilty or worry about it too much, because that's just how they've always done things.

—And they're probably raised to believe kidnapping and eating people is a great skill to have.

We said nothing.

—Dam.

—Yeah?

—Let's not raise ours like that.

—Our what?

—Our kid.

—Our kid?

I roared.

—What kid?

Gu kept a straight face.

—It might happen one day, you know, once things settle down.

—A kid doesn't just 'happen'. I'm not the Virgin Mary!

—One day, I mean someday, I'd like to be a father. I've never really had a dream before, but Noma—

Gu said it. *Noma*. It was the first time he'd said it since it happened.

—He told me his dream was to be the bestest dad in the world and I realised, I want that.

—To be the bestest dad?

—Yeah. You know, I was kind of jealous of him. I'd totally

forgotten, but it all came back to me a few days ago. Noma's dream, me thinking it was cool, you back then, me back then. I remember everything clearly.

Gu had entrusted me with Noma's dream.

—Hey, if we ever do have a kid, let's not leave them anything.

—You mean debt?

—Debt, money, any of it. Let's give them everything while we're still around.

I agreed without hesitating.

What is a human?

I asked, eating Gu. Am I a criminal? A psycho? A deviant? The devil? Am I even human? Children humanise objects, and adults objectify humans. The passage from childhood into adulthood is what keeps the world going round. Human beings are up for sale. They kill and eat anything. They lie and cheat. They have the power to ruin or save a life. They believe in God. And they use that God to their advantage. They undergo surgeries and take pills to stave off death. They cook with fire. And before they figured out how to tame the fire, they ate the flora and fauna raw. In prehistoric times, humans would have turned to cannibalism whether starving or sated. They would have hungered for her hand, his foot, their face, genitals. They would have eaten it all out of reverence, out of love. Is that primitive? Are we any better? We put a price on human life and erect hierarchies. Is money power? Is wealth nothing more than the survival of the fittest? Are we any more civilised than animals? An animal's power is hereditary. The strong devour the weak with jaws and claws. Money is also hereditary. The heirs prey on the poor. Without money, those who deserve to live, die. With money, those who deserve to die, thrive.

Why did Noma die?

Why did Auntie?

Why Gu?

Are car accidents, illness or poverty valid reasons for death? Do the enlightened accept the fact of death with composure? If they do, let me never reach enlightenment. I can come to terms with my own death, but I cannot come to terms with the death of a loved one. I'm still here, living through the pain of losing someone I love. The pain of getting left behind is seared into my soul. Let me be the one to leave. I found him hiding exactly thirty steps from the phone booth, his body a mess of wounds and bruises. Gu's eyes were bloodshot, his nose crushed, his front teeth missing. I asked him again and again if he was in pain, if he was in great pain. He said nothing. I collapsed onto the street clutching his body, picturing him taking those final thirty steps until dawn broke. His dying will, his body, his spirit. I wanted to claw into my skull and yank my brain out, anything to make it stop.

Gu died on the street.

What killed him?

Do I want to be human?

●

Dam's tongue is lapping at my face like she's trying to make out with me. Then she softly sinks her teeth into my cheek, tears streaming down hers. She cries out my name.

—Gu! Why do you hurt me? Why do you make me suffer?

She has never said those words before.

It's said that many evils escaped when Pandora opened her box, so why was hope there? I wish you'd got to hear this story. It was there because hope is a dangerous, slippery thing that faces the future. It makes you greedy, pulling in both anticipation and frustration like a mirage. I lived hopelessly, but until my very last breath, I lived. Because of you, Dam. I can live in a hopeless world, but I can't live in a world without you. Death is a place without you.

The day it happened, I was building the first pier in the river winding around the village. Mr Jang asked if I had ever seen the old bridge, and I nodded.

—The village used that bridge for nearly fifty years.

My mother crossed it to her wedding, and my daughter crossed it to university in Seoul.

I was picturing those five decades when a van crossed the new bridge. The bastards got out and carted me to some unknown location. I was beaten to a pulp. They used violence to break me, to make me into their puppet. As my mind slipped between memory and truth, I saw her at fifteen: Dam, caught between childhood and adulthood, standing on a street corner in a white blouse, chequered skirt, and nibbling at her hangnail. She was jogging in place to keep warm and rubbing her cheeks, waiting for me. Whether sold off, killed, whatever, I wanted to see her before losing the part of me that could remember her. The moment the van door opened, I ran for my life. I bolted down the stairs, but the sharks got me and laid into me hard. I tumbled down the remaining steps, flying into the street where neon signs burned my eyes. The world was spinning – people, buildings, cars, all becoming one. Even flat on my back, I fought like hell to keep from being hauled off. A thousand blows past feeling pain or fear, I found myself running straight into an oncoming car. I just kept going. I could have been crawling by that point, who knows, but I wouldn't give up.

—Go on. Catching you'll be a piece of cake!

They were right, but I couldn't give up. I had to reach Dam. Everything went. I could hear only my own breath, see only white and black. Crawling down a dark alley, I found a park with a phone booth and picked up the receiver.

—Dam. I see trees, trees that have stood here forever. Dam, you've waited so long. I tried so hard to reach you, but . . .

*

Fuck off.

Those were the words. The words I muttered to you before we became friends.

Back then, your tears used to piss me off. Back then, I picked on you to get close to you, to catch your eye, to make you aware of me, to mark my existence on yours. I could've been kind, but I was scared you'd return a blank stare. I was scared that my 'hello' would be left hanging in the air and you wouldn't even bother saying it back. I wanted the real you, not the perfunctory greetings you gave everyone else. I wanted you to snap at me for pulling your hair and then tease you some more, stretching the sweetness of the moment like a rubber band. But you didn't snap. You cried, and I got lost. I ended up angry at the butterflies in my stomach for hurting you. They hurt you throughout our relationship. Even now, they're still hurting you. Is that what love is? Is it like that for other people? There's so much I don't know.

Dam, you fool.

Enough. You've done everything you can. Wrap up the funeral and start living. You have to live for a long, long time.

You're here, and I'm here. I can only be where you are.

Look outside. I can only look outside if you do.

I can only live if you do.

Dam.

You fool.

In life, I believed the dead are reunited. Even if a realm like heaven or paradise didn't exist, there would be a place where, like a sieve separating the wheat from the chaff, the heavy is kept behind, allowing through nothing but the light. Our souls would roam, freed from their mortal coils. And people, knowing both life and death, would choose to live with the kindness they couldn't find on Earth. I never believed death dissolves loneliness or sadness, but without a body to get hungry or sick, without money to buy or own things, wouldn't you be free of material desires? The idea makes death and parting with my loved ones easier, because even in death, we might meet again. I'll wait, quietly, without pleading or rushing. I've heard that time is relative, and I hope that a hundred years on Earth feels like ten days in the afterlife. I want to believe in a place where after waiting only ten days, I get to see you again.

Yet I can't find a single trace of Noma or Auntie.

Yet you are here.

I'm with you, but you can't tell. I guess one of us isn't here, but now, watching you choke down my flesh and crying out in agony, I ask myself: what does any of it matter? Whether I'm here or not is a matter of feeling, and I'm dead. What does a dead man know about feeling, anyway? Yet I can feel. I am feeling you.

Auntie might be with the person she needs the most.

Noma with the person who matters most.

Like me, here, with you.

That's my truth now,

and I have to hold on to it.

●

Even if you die right this second, there's no guarantee we'll meet again.

I mean, I still can't find Noma or Auntie.

Will we meet again in another incarnation? Who knows? I came into the world and left it, but a rebirth hasn't yet happened. Will I come back to love a different you? Would you love a different me? It's hard to say. I can't picture you as anyone but the you I love, and I'm not sure I could love another you. I don't want to lose my memories of loving you in this life, but now I want only for you to live a long life remembering me and to watch over you through it. And when one day, after living and living, your tired body finally gives up, I want us to be together again as spirits or whatever's next. Only after you've lived a long, fulfilling life. Only then.

If you must die, I hope it's a thousand years from now.
I want to feel you for a thousand years.
Being dead, I can wait for you.
For millennia.

Author's Note

With previous books, I always had a sentence in mind for the postscript. This time, there isn't one. It feels like I've eaten a huge loaf of rye bread without leaving behind a single crumb. When it comes to this novel, I have no lingering thoughts or feelings. I feel emptied.

I spent the whole month of January hardly ever going outside, just holed up in my room, writing the story of Gu and Dam. It feels like the new year hasn't started yet, like it might never come, like last winter never happened and everything was a dream . . . Even though I'm the author, it doesn't feel like I wrote this story. I reviewed the proofs with this strange feeling.

Whenever I felt tired or unhappy while writing, I would slump like a pile of laundry and listen to 'Genesis' by 9 and the Numbers. This song is a little over three minutes long, but I would often put it on repeat and listen for over an hour, trying not to think about anything. Those were lonely, precious hours. Looking back, the memory of listening to that song is more vivid than the memory of writing this book.

In the past, I used to smile at the thought of tearing off

my lover's flesh and nibbling on it. In my mind, my lover's flesh was as chewy and sweet as a rice cake. Love made such acts of imagination possible, and imagination made that love possible. While writing, I often looked back on those times.

Many days, even while loving, I thought, *I want to love.* Even while writing, I thought, *I want to write.* Even while clearly being alive, I got lost in the thought, *I want to live.* So what am I doing? I don't know, but loving and writing are the best things for me right now. Maybe I'll find something better as I go on, but for now, I want to live without knowing anything better for as long as I can.

March 2015
Sitting in a chair for one
Choi Jin-young

About the Author

Choi Jin-young is one of South Korea's best-known authors. Her career started when she won the Silcheon Literature Debut Author Award in 2006. She has since won many more, including the Hankyoreh Literary Award, Shin Dong-yup Literary Prize, Baek Shin-ae Literature Award, Manhae Prize for Literature and, most recently, the Yi Sang Literary Award.

This brazen book was created by

Publisher: Romilly Morgan
Junior Commissioning Editor: Jane Link
Senior Editor: Alex Stetter
Editorial Assistant: Emily Campbell
Creative Director: Mel Four
Cover Designer: Micaela Alcaino
Copyeditor: Séan Costello
Typesetter: Six Red Marbles UK
Production Controller: Sarah Parry
Sales: Sammy Luton and Isobel Smith
Publicity & Marketing: Ailie Springall and Charlotte Sanders